A Body Among the Roses

Mrs. Lillywhite Investigates

BOOK FOUR

Emily Queen

A Body Among the Roses

ISBN- 978-1-953044-24-2

First Edition

Printed in the U.S.A.

Table of Contents

CHAPTER ONE

Rosemary Lillywhite bit her lip, pushed a lock of golden hair off her forehead, and frowned as she assessed the canvas perched on her easel. Somehow, no matter which shades she used or how meticulous were her brushstrokes, she couldn't seem to bring the colors of Cyprus to life in front of her. Not, at least, as vibrantly as she remembered them.

She'd been trying now for the two months since she'd returned to the London flat she had shared with her late husband, Andrew, who had died nearly a year before. Rosemary glanced at the stacks and rows of canvases already covered with images of what was supposed to have been a relaxing, cathartic holiday on the Isle of Love.

The vacation hadn't gone off as planned. Instead, she'd returned with more grief in her heart than when she'd left, and even though her friends had helped her solve a murder during their stay, finding Cecily's killer hadn't eased the shock of losing another person close to Rosemary's family.

"If only," she said aloud, wishing vehemently that she could capture the image of a golden sunset against a cerulean sea that swam behind her eyes. It seemed that if she could manage that, she might be able to put the whole sordid affair behind her.

Rosemary paced the room—the office Andrew had used for his private detective business and which she was contemplating turning into an art studio—shuffling her bare, paint-splattered feet across the cloth protecting the plush oriental rug underneath. She supposed she *had* turned it into a studio, if only a makeshift one, though her thoughts kept wandering back to the nameplate tucked into Andrew's top desk drawer. It read 'Rosemary Lillywhite, Private Investigator', but whether she was going to remove it from its hiding place and display it prominently on top of the desk was a decision yet to be made.

Doing so would mean declaring to the world—a world where women weren't expected to do such things—that she was a true detective. She wasn't certain she was ready to take that on, though it would be considered a boon for the equal rights movement still raging even after the fairer sex had demanded the ability to vote.

There were, Rosemary decided, limits to her willingness to further the cause.

"Madam," came a voice from the doorway, "your tea." Wadsworth, the butler, looked for a clean place to set down the tray and, finding none suitable enough for his tastes, raised an eyebrow at his mistress.

Rosemary pulled the protective cover off a small table and settled in to enjoy a quiet cuppa. "Wadsworth?" she said thoughtfully, a question in her voice. Unable to bring herself to actually ask it, she waved a hand. "Never mind."

Nodding once, the butler turned and left the room, closing the door softly behind him. Whatever was on his mistress's mind, it wasn't his place to pry, and so he didn't. When he was forced to return a few moments later, he found her sitting in the same position she'd been when he left, the full cup of tea going cold in her hand.

"Madam," Wadsworth said, rousing Rosemary from her reverie, "you have a phone call waiting in the parlor. It's Mrs. Woolridge." His tone indicated she ought to put a spring in her step, for her mother wouldn't appreciate being kept waiting.

Quickly, Rosemary hurried up the stairs from the ground-floor office and reached for the receiver before sitting down in front of the telephone. "Hello, Mother," she said, and was treated to an earful in return.

"Are you there, Rose?" Evelyn spoke loudly as if unsure she could be heard. "Is that you?"

"Yes, Mother. Who else were you expecting?"

"It's a disaster. All is gone to rack and ruin! I can't believe your father is so daft. How will I ever show my face again? Your father. I gave him one simple task," Evelyn Woolridge spouted, her words becoming tangled in her irritation. "You will come, won't you?"

Rosemary sighed. "Slow down. I can't understand a thing you're saying."

"Whatever do you mean?" Evelyn cried. "I've been perfectly clear. It's a disaster. When can you get here?"

"*What* is a disaster, exactly?" Rosemary demanded, recalling the last conversation she'd had with her mother and attempting to put the scattered pieces of Evelyn's ramblings into a sensible order.

Speaking slowly, as though Rosemary were a child, Evelyn explained. "The tea, Rosemary. The tea. You do remember me telling you about the Society for the Protection of Euphorbia Villosa, don't you?" Without waiting for an answer, she continued. "I've been put in charge, and this is the first event I'm to host. I asked your father to post the invitations two weeks ago. They were all tied up in two parcels, and he's managed only to post one. The rest he left in the boot of his car. I can't imagine what he must have been thinking!"

It didn't come as much of a shock to Rosemary, though now that she understood the situation, her mother's irritation made more sense.

"Perhaps you should have asked one of the maids or your butler to attend to the posting," Rosemary mused. "You know how absentminded Father can be. He'd forget to eat breakfast if you didn't remind him."

Evidently, that wasn't the response Evelyn was looking for, because she began to rant once more, and this time her ire was directed at Rosemary. "Absentmindedness is no excuse. He's a grown man; he ought to be able to remember the simplest of instructions. I find your soft spot for his shenanigans infuriating. The worst part is, he obviously made it to the post office, because he sent out half the invitations. Now, as chairwoman, it's on me to fill the empty seats."

Evelyn had, indeed, mentioned her newest protective endeavor in weekly missives that Rosemary had scanned cursorily as they'd gone on for quite some length. She'd declined reading through lists of the ladies who'd joined

4

the society—most of whom Rosemary considered quite frivolous and downright silly—but she couldn't—and wouldn't—say as much to her mother.

"Now," Evelyn demanded, "I need you to fill a seat—several, in fact—so bring as many people as you can. Your brother intends to invite Vera, of course, so she can't count for you." The name Vera came out sounding like a slur, and to that, Rosemary did take great offense.

"Mother," she sighed, "would it kill you to be nice to Vera? She's been my most trusted friend since we were children, you're close to her mother, and now she and Freddie are a couple." Rosemary ticked off several good reasons why Evelyn's attitude was inappropriate, to say the least. "She's part of the family in more ways than one already. What could she possibly have done to deserve this sudden spate of animosity?"

Evelyn balked. "Nothing whatever, dear. Vera's a lovely girl. Whether she's right for your brother is another matter altogether, but I'll try to keep an open mind." Her tone had taken on a lightness Rosemary recognized not as acquiescence, but an attempt to end the conversation.

She sighed again and, realizing there was no getting out of a trip to Pardington, vowed to further defend Vera when she had her mother's full attention.

"I'll be there as soon as possible, of course, and I'll see what I can do about filling some of your empty seats," she promised.

"Thank you, dear," Evelyn said, as if there were ever a question that, when faced with a family crisis—no matter how immaterial Rosemary thought it might be—she wouldn't rise to the occasion. "Your sister is here, and little Nelly of course. Leonard will arrive in time for the fête, or so I've been told. I'll put her on seating charts, and you can handle the rearrangements … or perhaps—" Evelyn continued to think out loud, for once, evidently, forgetting her strict rule about keeping all telephone calls to under five minutes.

Evelyn would change her mind twelve times before Rosemary arrived anyway, so she tuned her mother out and began making a mental list of people she could invite to fill those empty seats. The Redberrys from next door, of course. Abigail was the type to enjoy an afternoon among the hoity-toity country set, even if her husband, Martin, would be bored silly.

Long after Evelyn disconnected the line with a parting demand to "Get here as fast as you can," Rosemary racked her brain for more friends who might be willing to travel all the way out to Pardington. Unfortunately, she realized, she'd lost touch with so many of the couples who only served to remind her that she was now without a husband of her own.

"I'm really very sorry, Rose." Abigail Redberry's reply had come out on a sigh. "Martin is attending some sort of symposium to do with his work, and I'm to tag along. I do wish you and your mother good luck with the Euphorbia … whatever it was."

Her surest bet out of the running, Rosemary opened her address book and scanned through the list. Agatha Bainsbury, she remembered, had taken to clucking her tongue and shaking her head every time her eye fell on the new widow. For that reason, Rosemary decided, she would continue to avoid the woman at all costs. Besides which, Agatha's husband was possessed of a wandering eye.

Two minutes too late, she remembered Pansy Dalrymple's penchant for mindless prattle and her obsession with detailing her every vagrant thought. Strike that couple off the list.

Maybe there had been other reasons besides her tragic loss for letting go of some friendships. With finality, Rosemary closed her address book and stashed it back in the drawer.

Despite her reticence, Rosemary knew Evelyn expected her to deliver, and she thought for a moment that perhaps Max might be a willing participant, but then shook her head decidedly no. "I think it's best to learn a lesson from Pandora and leave the lid on that particular box," she said aloud.

Max was Maximilian Whittington, a handsome CID detective who had been Andrew's dearest comrade. Now, he was the man who threatened to wake Rosemary from her mourning period. Guilt at the thought of betraying Andrew's memory had tamped that hope back down to the bottommost places of her heart, and she'd been forced to tell Max that their relationship—if there were ever to be one—would have to be put on hold until she'd fully healed.

As if that hadn't been enough for her to deal with, Max wasn't the only one vying for her affections. There was Teddy Barton to consider, and Frederick's longtime chum Desmond Cooper, towards whom Rosemary had fostered an unrequited childhood crush. As her brother Frederick's best mate, Desmond would likely attend the party at Woolridge House, and having all three men there would make things more awkward than they already were. *If that's even possible*, Rosemary thought to herself as she placed another phone call.

"I need your help." Rosemary echoed her mother's plea so convincingly, she grimaced in chagrin.

"And so you shall have it," Vera Blackburn replied without hesitation, somehow managing to sound as though doing whatever Rosemary asked would be the highlight of her life. "What's happened? You sound tense."

Leave it to Vera to notice her melancholy even over the phone. "You're not going to like it," Rosemary said, expecting to take the shine off Vera's generous mood. "It involves a heaping dose of the incomparable Evelyn Woolridge."

"Oh, you must be talking about the SPEV tea party. I've already been told I'm expected to attend. You know, your brother has become quite presumptuous," Vera said, not seeming the least bit bothered by the fact. Quite the contrary, actually. Ever since sharing a long-anticipated kiss in Cyprus, Vera and her new beau had become inseparable despite Frederick having to spend most of his time in the country, running the family business alongside Rosemary's father.

That he took his position seriously was a testament to how much he'd grown up from the careless boy he'd once been, and Rosemary was prouder than he knew. She simply couldn't voice her opinion to Frederick, or he'd balk and protest, claiming he was only doing his familial duty. It was more than that, but Rosemary knew she'd have to let him come to that conclusion on his own.

"Perhaps I'll be able to impress your mother," Vera continued, a tinge of worry in her voice.

"Since when have you cared for my mother's opinion of you?" Rosemary asked, knowing full well the reason for her friend's change of perspective.

With a harrumph, Vera retorted, "Don't be daft, Rosie dear. I may have been a staunch supporter of the suffrage movement, and yes, I enjoy thumbing my nose at authority, but that doesn't have to mean I should be thrilled that my beau's mother can't stand the sight of me."

"I don't think her feelings have changed towards you," Rosemary said, "so much as I think she simply hasn't accepted it's not Lionel you'll be marrying."

Neither her friend nor her brother had mentioned marriage thus far, so Rosemary held her breath while she waited to see what Vera might say on the subject.

Vera paused momentarily, swallowed the lump in her throat and replied, "Well, there isn't anything I can do about that, now is there?"

There wasn't, and the subject quickly changed, as it always did when Rosemary's other, deceased brother's name came up in conversation. Had he survived, he and Vera would have been wed long ago; instead, Vera had rejected the idea of tying herself to any man and had spent the last few years as a single woman.

"I can put on a show and pretend to get along; I'm an actress, after all. Nevertheless, I intend to win her over this weekend. Now, who are you inviting and what are you going to wear? Never mind, I know you haven't given that a bit of thought. I'll take care of it, and I'll pick you up. We'll go together," Vera said and, without waiting for Rosemary's reply, hung up the phone.

CHAPTER TWO

A mixture of pleasure and pain washed over Rosemary's senses when the car turned in at the drive leading to Woolridge House. She hadn't been home since the mix-up at the Bartons' anniversary party, when she'd had to solve a murder for which Frederick was the prime suspect. Just as it had then, the sight of her childhood home brought forth a plethora of emotions that crashed over her like ocean waves.

She heard Vera's quick intake of breath and noted that her friend had stopped the incessant chattering that had filled the hour-long drive. Even this far from the house, there was evidence of Evelyn's touch. Not a single rut marred the drive, and the lawn had been ruthlessly trimmed into submission. "The grounds look lovely, wouldn't you agree?" she murmured to Vera, who merely nodded.

When Rosemary turned to peer at her friend, it was to find a mere shell of the vibrant, self-confident woman who usually stared back at her. This Vera was practically shaking, biting her lip so hard it was a wonder she didn't break flesh. "Relax, it will all be fine in the end. I promise." Rosemary patted Vera's hand and smiled encouragingly.

"Here goes nothing," Vera said, taking a deep breath and arranging her face into a neutral expression when the car finally rolled to a stop outside the front door.

Before Rosemary could reach for the door handle, it opened, and Bertram, the Woolridges' butler, ushered the women inside. "Miss Rose, Miss Vera," he greeted them, without the usual twinkle in his eye. "Your sister is in the dining room. I recommend you join her," he said, his eyes flicking to the closed parlor door with unease.

A maid scuttled past, her arms loaded with bolts of cloth, and kept her gaze to the ground. A rustle from the parlor had her picking up the pace, and she disappeared down the corridor leading to the service staircase.

"We'll do that, then," Rosemary replied, and headed towards the dining room. "Oh dear," she said to Vera on the way. "Mother must be in a right state."

"But Papa," Rosemary's sister, Stella, pleaded as Rosemary entered, "you've got to do something. I'm bored to absolute tears, and every time I rearrange the seating chart to Mother's specifications, she changes her mind and I have to start all over. It's an exercise in futility, I tell you!"

"Oh, wonderful, your sister is here," Cecil Woolridge said, turning his attention away from his youngest daughter without replying to her complaints. "She'll know what to do." He kissed Rosemary on the cheek and then repeated the gesture with Vera.

"It's lovely to see you, dear," he said warmly. "I'm off to the office, but I'll tell Frederick you've arrived."

He winked at her, bringing a flush of color to Vera's cheeks. Rosemary noted that her spine straightened infinitesimally, as though the approval of at least one Woolridge was enough to bring back a shred of her usual confidence.

"Thank you, Mr. Woolridge," Vera replied, pleased.

"Cecil, dear, is good enough," he said. The way her father skulked out of the dining room and beat a hasty retreat through the front door, Rosemary suspected he was keen to get away without his wife's notice. She could hardly blame him and turned to Stella for answers.

"What on earth is going on?" Rosemary embraced her sister. "I've never seen the house in such a state of disarray." It looked as if Evelyn were preparing for a siege. One table held at least thirty silver candlesticks, and Rosemary wondered what on earth her mother could be thinking. "Isn't this an afternoon event? You could light up half of London with those."

"That's what I said, but do you think she listened? She's finally decided they're unnecessary and must be returned—just like most of the rest of what's stuffed in here. Father has done his level best to avoid her for the past few days, and she's relegated Nelly to the nursery because she's afraid he'll make a mess. Irony never was Mother's friend. He's dying to see you, by the way," Stella said, a twinkle in her eye. "He says you're the best auntie in the whole world."

Rosemary grinned. "I suspect that has something to do with the boxes of chocolates I always remember to carry with me."

"It's more than that," Stella said, her lips twitching.

"What is it?" Rosemary's eyes narrowed. "You know

you can't fool me, and you're grinning like the Cheshire cat." She appraised her sister carefully, noted the way she held her hand over her abdomen, then exchanged a glance with Vera who raised an eyebrow and nodded. "You're going to have another baby, aren't you?"

"Yes!" Stella exclaimed, her face lit with happiness. "Isn't it grand?"

Of course it was, and Rosemary wouldn't begrudge her sister a moment of glee, no matter how much it made her realize just how far off track her own life had got. "Congratulations, dear sister," she said, embracing Stella. "I do hope this one is a girl," she whispered into her sister's hair, "and if it is, I think you'll find yourself simply swimming in little pink dresses. Right, Vera?"

"More than she could ever possibly wear, I'd wager."

"Speaking of wagers," Stella replied, "I've just won ten pounds from our fool of a brother. I bet him you'd guess my news within ten minutes of your arrival, and you did! Now, as long as this ridiculous tea party goes off without a hitch and Mother calms down a bit, I'll be the happiest woman in the world. You know, she won't let me do anything except sit here, even though the doctor said I should carry on as usual."

"That sounds just like Mother," Rosemary mused. "Tell me, what has put her and the house into such a state?" she asked, once more looking around at the condition of the dining room.

Stella rolled her eyes. "It started when she decided to turn the tea into a fancy luncheon and we had to talk her out of the notion. That took three days and a lot of weeping. Finally, Mother called Mrs. Shropshire, and they've decided to do a traditional high tea."

Mrs. Shropshire owned a tearoom in Pardington and was possessed, to Rosemary's way of thinking, with precisely the right sensibility to counteract the worst flights of fancy upon which Evelyn would inevitably embark.

"Meanwhile, she had borrowed warming pans and serving dishes from ... well, quite frankly, I'm not certain where, and has had to hire a driver and lorry to return everything from whence it came."

Stella seemed to take undue delight in her mother's discomfiture. Probably, Rosemary supposed, a direct result of withstanding Evelyn's unwarranted disapproval all these years.

"Then, there was the matter of the seating. Once committed to inviting all and sundry, it became clear our supply was woefully short. Mother called *your* mother, Vera, and they've pulled what they can from her house, and also from Barton Manor. Mrs. Barton is still so grateful for your part in solving the murder investigation that she'd probably loan Mother the Hope Diamond should she be so lucky as to have it in her possession."

Having been called upon to *prevent* the murder at Barton Manor and failing to do so, Rosemary felt Mrs. Barton's gratitude was misplaced. Her frown at the thought went unnoticed.

"Thankfully," Stella said, reaching up to pick at the collar of her dress, "between the three households, there are enough formal dining chairs to seat a small army. Let me tell you, that was the most dreadfully boring day of my life, but we finally managed to put together a quaint sort of mismatched look that coordinates perfectly with Mrs. Shropshire's collection of vintage teapots. Most of this"—Stella motioned to the mess—"is waiting to be picked up, but the lorry hasn't arrived, and now Mother is tending to her pack of hens in the parlor, hoping against hope that they'll be gone before the hired help comes to retrieve the unnecessary supplies."

Looking around to make certain Evelyn was firmly out of hearing, Rosemary had to ask, "What is *Euphorbia villosa,* and why is Mother so determined to protect it?"

Stella's eyes lit up brightly with humor. She pulled Rosemary and Vera into the far corner of the dining room where she could explain without fear of Evelyn overhearing, and still she spoke in a stage whisper.

"A month or two ago, there was a young man traveling hereabouts, called himself a botanist. That's the study of plants."

Rosemary waved a hand. "Yes, I'm familiar with the concept."

"He made quite a stir around these parts. Handsome fellow, and fervent in his pursuit of science. Turned more than a few heads."

For the first time since arriving, Vera showed a ghost of her former self. "This is all on account of a man? Fancy that!"

"Oh no, he was merely the catalyst." Stella grinned and spoke a little more loudly. "Round the neighborhood he went, knocking on doors and asking permission to roam the gardens and borders looking for *Euphorbia villosa*, a herbaceous plant, he said, that was on the verge of extinction."

Rosemary snapped her mouth shut, as it had dropped open in surprise. "A plant? She's doing all of this for a plant?"

"A plant better known by its common name," Stella announced. "We're throwing a tea party for the Society for the Protection of Hairy Spurge."

Vera snorted, and Rosemary gave in to the urge to giggle. "Hairy spurge?"

"That's the common name, and it grates on Mother's nerves when I call it that. It's not just Mother, either. We have a whole contingency of hairy spurge protectors on our hands. Most of the younger set have entered the fray, and that's what has Mother whipped into a frenzy. She's concerned they're planning to stage a coup in order to take control of the entire endeavor."

"A hairy spurge coup." Vera fell into another fit of laughter. "Only in Pardington."

Stella went on to mention that the project had grown to include more than just saving an endangered plant, but was interrupted when the parlor door opened, and the sound of shuffling feet in the corridor wafted into the room. "I'd better go and say hello," Rosemary said, and strode towards the door.

"Go around the other way, and hurry. She won't want those women peeking in here," Stella warned. "They're unaware of just how far 'round the bend' this whole affair has gone."

Rosemary and Vera left Stella to her lists, then bustled into the kitchen, where the mess had also intruded, and down another corridor until they found themselves back in the entrance hall surrounded by the oddest assortment of women to ever enter Woolridge House as a group.

Half the protection society seemed to be made up of women closer to her mother's age; the other half were

Rosemary's, though they weren't dressed anything like the twenty-somethings of London she'd grown accustomed to. Some sort of hybrid sect, they wore drop-waist dresses and cloche hats, but each one sported a mane of long hair rather than the cropped bobs most of the bright young set had adopted. No sheer stockings on this bunch, either, and not a knee in sight, though they all appeared to have impeccable taste in shoes.

Recognizing a few of the younger set from her school days and stifling a snort, Vera put on her serious face—the one reserved for discussions on such matters as the proper ratio of gin to tonic—and prepared to greet Evelyn.

"Oh, Rosemary, you're here. How lovely," Rosemary's mother said as though she hadn't called and demanded her daughter sprout wings if that would get her to Pardington more swiftly. "And you've brought Vera." Evelyn had no further comment regarding that detail, and barely made eye contact with Vera while kissing her, perfunctorily, on each cheek.

"Well, if it isn't the prodigal daughter." The tone indicated the surprise wasn't as pleasant as Mrs. Woolridge had implied. Rosemary squinted and searched her memory for a younger version of the narrow face and deep-set eyes. She'd nearly pulled up the name just as Vera's elbow made contact with her ribs in a sharp jab.

"Queenie Cole." The consummate actress, Vera mimicked the woman's acerbic tone perfectly and caused Rosemary to swallow a giggle. "It's been an absolute age."

Four women nearer her own age crowded around

Queenie, who lived up to her name when she raised her chin in the air and cast a sidelong glance at her entourage, then slid her eyes back to Rosemary and Vera as if in challenge.

"It's Queenie Baker now," she said as though in landing a husband she'd accomplished an insurmountable feat. "We're surprised you deigned to attend our little protection society fête at all, aren't we, ladies?"

As if rehearsed, the others nodded in unison, all but one of them with the same haughty air as Queenie's. It wasn't surprising that Franny Cole followed along after her cousin, Queenie—she always had, and probably always would. Once Rosemary's memory unlocked, the rest of the names came flooding back. Names she remembered from the long missives her mother sent when there was news of note from Pardington. Weddings and funerals always made the grade.

Olive Adams wore a dress nearly identical to Queenie's, but there the resemblance ended, for Olive was several inches shorter and carried at least a full stone more weight. By contrast, her face bare of makeup, Minnie Kitteridge needed another woman in there with her to fill out her frock. Unless time changed them, these were two women similarly suited to do another's bidding, having never possessed minds of their own as far as Rosemary remembered. Only the fifth member wasn't quite so keen to turn up her nose at Evelyn Woolridge's daughter.

How Elsie—formerly Carlyle and now Fletcher—had become connected with such a vapid circle of friends was a mystery, indeed. She alone allowed the corner of her mouth to turn up into a semi-smile at Vera's spunk, though it disappeared from her face following a harsh look from Queenie.

One more vague recollection surfaced, just a snippet, really, of Queenie having been the victim of a malicious prank during their school days. Someone had laced her tea with laxatives, creating an inescapable, embarrassing situation for the ever-composed Queenie, and the culprit had never been caught or brought to justice. Rosemary made a note to ask Vera later if she could supply more detail, then promptly forgot all about it.

"I see not much has changed around here," Vera said lightly, though the set of her jaw let Rosemary know that she'd have loved nothing more than to see the queen bee rousted from her throne. Furthermore, Rosemary suspected her friend might have made a snide comment about hairy spurge, had Evelyn not been standing right there.

"Yes, well," Queenie sneered, "some things are different. We're all, except for Franny, of course, married women now." She snorted, and it was another example of how uncharitable she could be, even to her own cousin. Rosemary could practically feel Franny bristle. The glare she sent at Queenie's back spoke volumes, but instead of defending herself, she allowed the other biddies-in-the-making to snicker as though it was a normal occurrence.

Evelyn's brow furrowed in disapproval, and she exchanged a glance with one of the older contingent—a thick rope of a woman with chiseled cheekbones that sat high on her sun-kissed face.

"Now, Queenie," the formidable woman said,

speaking both for Evelyn and herself it seemed, "marriage isn't the only path to happiness, you know. Some of us find fulfillment in other pursuits, and a good thing, too, because husbands aren't always forever."

The comment stung Rosemary, even though it wasn't aimed at her. She paled, and the woman, realizing her gaffe, sent an apologetic look in her direction. Queenie's look of perpetual disapproval shifted from Rosemary and Vera, and instead looked Evelyn's friend up and down.

"Yes, well, one has a better chance of keeping a husband when one takes care of one's appearance." Apparently, she didn't approve of women who wore trousers, particularly not trousers with soil-stained knees.

"Auntie Rose, Auntie Rose!" Tow-headed, and cherubic of face though not of manner, Stella's son Nelly barreled around the corner, nearly bowling over Queenie and her cluster of hangers-on. Another boy of about the same age, who Rosemary didn't recognize, entered the hall behind him. "You're here!" Nelly yelled.

Chattering a mile a minute, he clung to Rosemary's legs until she lifted him for a kiss on both cheeks. "There's my little man," she said. "You've grown so big!"

Rosemary smiled and gently set the boy back on his feet. "But you, young master Nelly, should go and apologize for nearly knocking Queenie off her feet. Running with such abandon was rather rude of you, you know."

Dutifully, Nelly's chubby legs carried him to the

group of women. "Sorry." To further impress the point, he patted Queenie on the knee. Rosemary waited for the inevitable sneer and was surprised when the woman bent down, smiled, and fingered one of Nelly's curls.

"You're forgiven, young sir." Straightening, she reached into her purse and pulled out a boiled sweet.

Nelly's eyes widened, his lips rounded. "Thank you," he said reverently when Queenie pressed the wrapped sweet into his pudgy fist, and he gave her leg a quick hug before he scampered off to eat his treat.

Rosemary thought she caught a flash of longing crossing Queenie's face, but then, it was hard to be around Nelly and not give in to a bit of yearning.

"Come on, Nigel," Elsie said to the other boy who, Rosemary deduced, must have been her son. "You can come back and play with Nelly another time. Now, where is Miss Amelia?"

Before the question left her lips, a young woman entered the entrance hall carrying a large bag overflowing with toys, her brow wrinkled into a worried expression. "I'm sorry, Mrs. Fletcher," she said, apologizing for the delay. "I had to search for Nigel's toy car; if we'd forgotten it, he would have been quite distraught later."

"Thank you, Amelia, you did just as you should have," Elsie replied, and the girl's face relaxed. Without the frown, Miss Amelia was possibly the most classically beautiful young woman Rosemary had ever seen, with dark, almost black, hair against fair skin, rosy cheeks, and bright green eyes. Without another word, Queenie and her friends made their exit, tittering the entire way out the door.

"I'm Beryl, by the way. Beryl Dixon. It's a pleasure," the woman who'd spoken sharply to Queenie said gruffly, her eyes carrying a silent apology for her earlier comment regarding husbands. "Your mother speaks very highly of you."

"Lovely to meet you too," Rosemary replied, flashing a sincere smile.

"I've no doubt you've a better head on your shoulders than that treacherous nincompoop," Beryl laughed, referring to Queenie. "The nerve of me, showing up at a meeting to protect an endangered plant and actually participating in some form of gardening."

Vera laughed. "It doesn't count as gardening when one hires out all of the manual labor, does it?" She said in another fair imitation of Queenie.

In reply, Beryl let out a guffaw. "No, it certainly doesn't."

To Evelyn, she offered a mild rebuke. "Once you let that bindweed take hold, you'll never get it out of your beds. It's positively pernicious, but now, I must be off. Evelyn, should you need anything else, you let me know, you hear?" She sent a meaningful glance towards the dining room door, making Rosemary wonder if she could see through it and to the mess on the other side.

CHAPTER THREE

"I had no idea Queenie and her flock of hens were members of the, um, society," Rosemary said once the locusts had cleared out of Woolridge House and she'd followed her mother back to the dining room. It hadn't escaped her attention that, if she hadn't chosen to go to London and attend art school, she herself might be spending her days worrying about the future of an oddly named plant. The thought was unsettling to say the least.

Evelyn sighed and wrung her hands together. "The lot of them will be the death of me. That woman hasn't a kind word to say to anyone, and Beryl is right. Not a one of them could tell a carrot from a cabbage as it grew, that I can assure you. However, not all women find the allure in city life and the gallivanting around you young girls do these days." She cast a sidelong glance towards Vera as the words tumbled from her lips.

"Furthermore, we can't afford to turn away willing members, especially those who are yet still young enough to carry on after the rest of us are gone."

"I don't understand. Carry on what? Saving the hairy spurge from extinction doesn't sound like a project to span lifetimes. Nor does a group of people swilling tea seem likely to do so." The comment popped out before Rosemary could clamp her lips shut to hold it in. Narrowing her eyes, Evelyn put on her loftiest tone.

"We shall hold a raffle to raise money. A small sum will go to fund Mr. Murray Alden's continued efforts to search the countryside for endangered plants." Evelyn puttered about while she talked, moving boxes to and fro in no discernible pattern. "Now that Queenie and her friends have joined our efforts, and now that we're seeing how much good we can do as a group, we're also turning our attention to the revitalization project."

Rosemary, without a clue what to do that her mother would consider helpful, sat down next to Stella and folded her hands on the table. Vera followed suit.

"What revitalization project?" Rosemary wanted to know.

Before Evelyn could open her mouth, Vera answered for her. "There's a new inn being built next to the tearoom in the village square, and there's even talk of putting in a small theater. My mother is extremely keen on the idea, and I believe she intends to invest some money in the project. With both Woolridge & Sons and Barton Enterprises based in Pardington, the population has increased significantly. All those workers need places to stay and things to do. Did you know they've begun construction on a housing tract just off the main road? It will mean more tax money, which will mean better roads and expansion."

Vera's knowledge of the intricacies of Pardington economics was news to Rosemary, and she stared at her friend with a wrinkled brow.

"Stop looking at me as if I've grown a second head. Frederick explained it all to me. He's very knowledgeable when it comes to these things," Vera said proudly, but Evelyn made a tut-tut noise and took the wind out of her sails.

"Frederick is an idealist, certainly. He doesn't always look at both sides of a thing," Evelyn said. "Working in service to a good family used to mean something."

For the next few minutes, Rosemary sat in stunned silence while her mother offered commentary on how the scarcity of good help had begun to put landed homes in jeopardy. Evelyn spoke with passion on the subject of how the new rows of smaller homes springing up in towns were necessary to generate tax money to balance the losses.

"Building an inn," Rosemary said, "suggests an expectation that guests will come to stay in Pardington."

"To do what?"

Evelyn slanted a hard look at an incredulous Vera.

"Going on holiday need not be a hedonistic experience. Pardington has much to offer those with more discerning tastes." The icy needles of Evelyn's tone dashed against Vera's hopes.

"I didn't mean—"

"Oh, I know what you meant. Nonetheless, I see no reason why caravanning families shouldn't stop and stay in Pardington a night or two, and maybe they would do, if they had a chance to take in a show. Who knows, maybe someone will come along and open up one of those jazz clubs you seem so enamored with."

Rosemary now shifted her disbelieving gaze towards her mother. "Since when did everyone in this house become so well versed in village business?"

"Dear," Evelyn replied, "I've lived with your father for thirty-odd years now, running this household, which is an entity in and of itself. One picks up a thing or two. As a great proponent of women's equality, I'm surprised at your disbelief in the fact that I possess an understanding of basic economic principles."

"That's not what I meant, Mother." Rosemary jumped to her own defense, unsure how the conversation had ended up skirting the topic of women's liberation. "I'm merely commenting on the fact that, until now, I've never heard either of you talk about such things."

Evelyn pierced her with a gaze. "One must keep up with current events, mustn't one?" It sounded as though she thought Rosemary was completely out of touch, which was a reversal of roles, to say the least. "And there's the lorry now, come to get these boxes," Evelyn said, her ears perking as the front door opened.

Except it wasn't, as Rosemary found out when Bertram ushered a bright-eyed, attractive man into the dining room. "Well, if it isn't the lady detective herself. And of course, her trusty fellow sleuth. Hello, Rosemary. Hello, Vera." He greeted them both with a kiss on the hand, though his lips lingered far longer on Rosemary's. "Lovely to see you both again."

"Likewise," Vera said, sliding her eyes in her friend's direction, a smirk playing around her lips. "Did you bring Grace with you?"

"No," Teddy Barton said, finally tearing his gaze away from Rosemary's. "My sister is busy with wedding plans, but she said to tell you hello, and that she'll call on you when she's in London next month. I've simply come to supervise the unloading of the chairs Mother sent down. She's quite partial to that Georgian set and says she doesn't trust the driver to properly unload them. Where should I point the men, Evelyn?"

Rosemary noted his use of her mother's first name and wondered just how close the two had become, given Evelyn's fascination with the idea of Teddy becoming Rosemary's next husband.

"The solarium, dear. I'll show you." She linked arms with Teddy and led him in that direction. When Rosemary and Vera followed, Stella took the opportunity to escape her menial task and accompanied them out.

At the back of the house, overlooking the garden, the solarium was one of Rosemary's favorite places to enjoy a quiet cup of tea or simply gaze at the gardens set against a backdrop of rolling hills. Now, she found the room transformed into a fitting place for the upper crust of Pardington to attend high tea and donate scads of money for the protection of weeds. And, of course, for the revitalization project.

Long, narrow, and filled with light, the solarium spanned most of the rear of the manor house. Linen-covered tables spread across the flagstones, some with chairs pulled up, some without. Crates were stacked along the wall, making Rosemary wonder what they could possibly contain considering the state of the dining room.

"She's gone positively batty," Stella said low enough so only the three of them could hear her. "Father says the cost of the food alone would have covered Mr. Alden's lodging for a year, and he'll be surprised if the venture breaks even."

"He said that to Mother?" Rosemary lifted an eyebrow.

Stella grinned and shook her head. "No. Father's much too shrewd to commit such utter folly. He claims he has work and tries to stay out of the way."

"Your father is a wise man," Vera pointed out, then linked her arm with Rosemary's as the three women returned inside. "It is, unfortunately, too late for us to beg off."

Not that Vera would have turned down any reasonable request from the woman who might, someday, become true family.

In the dining room, Teddy waited. The way his gaze settled on Rosemary made it obvious for what. "Be nice," Vera whispered as she disengaged and took Stella's arm instead. "We'll be … somewhere around, certainly."

Deserted in my hour of need, Rosemary thought as she turned to face the man who waited for a moment of her time. With Evelyn's commands echoing throughout the manor and the help bustling to carry out her wishes, the only quiet place in the house was to be found outside it. The pair settled on a bench nestled in a nook on the veranda.

"How have you been, Rose?" Teddy asked, enough sincerity in his voice that she felt certain he really wanted to know and wasn't simply using asking as an excuse to proposition her for a date.

"I'm well enough, I suppose," Rosemary replied. "Though I do wish I'd stop happening upon dead bodies." She voiced the complaint with a wry smile.

"I heard what took place in London, and then again during your holiday in Cyprus. Though, if what you want is to become a true lady detective, you're on the right track." He leaned back, lit a cigarette, took a long drag, and blew out a ring that floated into the air above his head like a smoky halo.

Rosemary balked. "Whoever said I wanted to become a true lady detective anyway? Did my mother put that notion in your head?" She rolled her eyes towards the heavens. The image of the nameplate still tucked into Andrew's top drawer came to mind, and she shook her head to rid herself of it.

"Evelyn Woolridge is the bee's knees," Teddy quipped, bemused but respectful.

"That she is," Rosemary said lightly. "I don't know how I got roped into helping with this fête, but it sounds as if the do might be a boon for Pardington if the prevention society can manage to raise enough money for their village square revitalization project. Though, part of the appeal of a small village is quaintness, and something tells me it won't remain quaint for long if we're inundated with outsiders."

"Progress for the sake of progress doesn't appeal to you?" Again, there was that bemused tone.

She sighed. "I suppose you're making a quip against women's rights. It seems as though I'm destined to be called a stuffed shirt on multiple occasions today."

"I said nothing of the sort. One has little to do with the other."

"Doesn't it, though?" Rosemary asked with a raised eyebrow.

"Perhaps, but that's neither here nor there at the

moment. I certainly wasn't questioning your dedication to the women's movement, nor do I wish to discuss politics. I came here to see you, Rose. Mother could have sent anyone along with the lorry driver." He leaned forward, his elbows resting on his knees, and pierced her with hopeful eyes.

His bold statement brought a flush of color to Rosemary's cheeks. She'd hoped that after several months, Teddy's interest in her might have waned so that perhaps they could have avoided this awkward conversation. She should have known her mother would make every attempt to keep the flame lit, even in her absence, and it seemed as though that was just what Evelyn had done.

"Stop, please," Rosemary pleaded. "I don't want to have to shoot you down, Teddy. I like you too much for that."

He took another drag of his cigarette, then rotated in his chair to stub it out in the soil of a planter overflowing with cosmos. When he turned back towards her, there was no anger in his eyes, only resignation.

"I'd like to be friends," she said softly.

"Your mother won't like that," Teddy replied. "She has her heart set on the two of us hitting it off. If I'm being honest, she's part of the reason I've kept you in the back of my thoughts."

Unsure of his meaning, Rosemary quirked an eyebrow.

"She's been very nurturing to me these last few months. I suspect she hasn't told you about our little chats. I also expect you think that's rather odd, me coming down here to converse with your mother."

When Rosemary tipped her head to one side rather than agree, he continued. "You're lucky, you and Freddie. He and I have become great pals, you know, and so I've been spending a bit of time at Woolridge House."

Rosemary shook her head. "I didn't know. Frederick hasn't mentioned anything about you, but then that's my brother for you. He's been rather a pill since he took up with Vera, though I doubt that has anything to do with it."

She suspected her brother still had it in his head that someday Rosemary would end up with Desmond, after all, and hadn't told her of his friendship with Teddy Barton out of worry she might toss Desmond over for a chance with Pardington's most eligible bachelor. "That still doesn't explain why, of all people, you enjoy spending time with my mother."

"She's a lovely woman. Quite the conversationalist and always ready to lend a sympathetic ear. You'd be surprised how hard it is to find anyone who doesn't think I've got no cause for complaints, but Evelyn knows that money doesn't necessarily buy happiness. I quite liked the idea of spending holidays here, of being part of a family like yours. However, when you said you didn't want to have to shoot me down, I have to admit I felt a pang of … well, relief, I suppose."

For a moment, Rosemary felt a sense of righteous indignation. She wasn't a prideful woman—didn't believe herself some grand prize—but she was still a woman, and hearing that Teddy was relieved to be rejected stung a little. Then, she burst out laughing.

"What?" he asked with a quizzical look as she

dissolved into giggles.

"I've heard men say that they'll never understand the way a woman thinks. I shall let you in on a little secret, Teddy Barton—there are times when we're a mystery to ourselves."

As Rosemary would say no more, Teddy had to be content with her response.

CHAPTER FOUR

Rosemary hadn't the chance to relay her conversation with Teddy to Vera before the time came to get ready for dinner, and even less opportunity to tell her during the preparations, because all Vera could talk about was Evelyn. It seemed the woman was capable of inspiring a myriad of emotions, because Vera's opinion of her was in almost direct opposition to Teddy's.

"What is wrong with what I'm wearing?" she asked, stomping back and forth in front of the wardrobe in Rosemary's old room, where one of the maids had hung the clothes from their cases. Despite there being a number of empty guest rooms, whenever the pair visited Woolridge Manor, they insisted upon staying in this room, as they always had during childhood and adolescence.

"Maybe I should have stayed at my mother's house instead of coming here. All I've managed to do is irritate yours, which is the precise opposite of my intention." Vera appraised every outfit she'd brought along and appeared to find fault with all of them.

"It's not your clothes, my dear. My mother is simply

having a hard time adjusting to the idea of you and Frederick as a couple. Combine that with the disaster of this fête, and what we have is an Evelyn volcano, ready to erupt. You just happen to be a suitable target in her eyes. Once she sees the two of you together, I think she'll change her tune."

"Well," Vera huffed, flopping down onto the bed, "I'm going to do everything in my power to make certain she does. Starting with a trip to the shops first thing tomorrow morning." Her mind made up, she set to picking out a dinner outfit, dressing for Frederick, as she worried nothing would please her possible future mother-in-law anyway.

Rosemary watched, bemused, as her friend, who had sworn off men mere days before finally succumbing to Frederick's charms, fretted over her appearance. "I thought you never wanted to settle down. I thought you wanted to be wild and free for the rest of your days."

Vera sent her a reproachful look. "We've been over this before, Rosie. And you know I wouldn't have got involved with your brother in the first place if I didn't think it was serious. That night on the beach, when he said all those things to me, I felt something stir inside. I thought that part of me—the part that wanted someone to grow old with—died with Lionel."

"For your sake, I'm glad that it didn't, and you should be as well."

Vera sat back down on the bed and rested her hand on her chin. "I know that, deep down, and honestly, it's sort of the best of both worlds with Frederick."

"Please don't tell me anything else. He's still my brother, you know."

"That's not what I meant; get your mind out of the gutter. What I meant was Freddie keeps things interesting. He's always willing to go off on whatever half-cocked adventure I've dreamed up. He likes to travel, have a good time, doesn't take life too seriously. I think that someday, if this comes to anything, he would make an excellent father and husband."

Having blurted her most secret thoughts, Vera backtracked. "It's entirely possible we'll tire of one another before the week is out and none of this will matter. But if I should decide to marry your brother, I expect to be welcomed into this family with open arms—by everyone, including your mother."

What Vera wanted, Vera usually got, and it didn't surprise Rosemary to see her get worked into a lather at the possibility that this time, she might not.

Only after rotating through all her own and most of Rosemary's dresses, Vera finally selected a modest yet fashionable black frock with only a few strips of fringe to lend a sense of whimsy.

"Are you sure it's not too much?" Nervously, Vera brushed her hands down over her hips.

"It's the bee's knees, now stop fussing," Rosemary replied. "You're not having a royal audience, after all. You've sat at our table countless times."

In the upstairs corridor, Stella was saying good night to Nelly, who pushed past his mother when he caught sight of Rosemary.

"Auntie!" he yelled excitedly and launched himself into her arms. Rosemary laughed and held him close, relishing the fresh baby scent that still lingered even though he was hardly a baby anymore.

"You're almost too big to do that, love."

"I'm a big boy now," Nelly replied proudly. "I caught some frogs today, and I didn't even need a net or Nan's help! Miss Vera, will you come down to the pond with me and Auntie tomorrow, like last time?"

Vera raised an eyebrow and said in a mock-serious tone, "I don't know, kid, last time you got mud in my hair."

"That was an accident," Nelly said, though his eyes flicked away guiltily. "I promise I won't do it again."

"Nelly," Stella said sternly, "I'm certain Auntie Rose and Miss Vera will find some time to play with you while they're here, but now it's dinner time, and we've got to go. Nan will take care of you." Nan was ancient, had acted as nanny for all the Woolridge children, and was almost a part of the family.

The boy appeared morose but did as he was told after squeezing Rosemary into one last hug.

"Why is he going to bed so early?" Rosemary asked. "Mother usually insists we all dine together."

Stella sighed as she led the way down the stairs. "Oh, Nelly is in a bit of trouble. He's discovered all the little nooks and crannies in this house—no thanks to Frederick—and he's been sneaking biscuits from the tin in the kitchen. Cook complained about the trails of crumbs and accused him of trying to lure in mice to keep as pets."

All three women shuddered at the thought before Stella continued.

"Yesterday, we found him climbing up one of the trellises out back. Mother threatened to tan his hide if he destroyed her climbing jasmine. I thought it best he have an early bedtime. Heaven knows what I'm going to do when there are two of them running around. Speaking of the devil, I believe I hear Freddie now," she said, swinging open the dining room door.

"Surely, Mother, you can't be serious." Frederick waved an already empty glass around as he spoke. "This whole thing is ludicrous. I know all the same people you know, save my London mates. Would you like me to fill a seat with my pal Smitty, who would chat up his own maiden aunt, or Munson, the perpetual spiller of drinks?" His curly blond hair dangled in front of his eye, and he brushed it aside impatiently while striding across the room towards Vera. He wrapped a protective arm around her waist and whispered something in her ear that sparked a wry smile.

"Frederick Woolridge, you had better wipe that look off your face right now," Evelyn retorted, "and watch your attitude." She glared in his direction, including Vera in her ire, and brought the mood in the room down a few more degrees.

"What's the trouble?" Rosemary asked, even though she had already discerned the reason for her mother's irritation.

"The trouble is," Evelyn said, still exasperated, "that none of you, save your sister"—she treated Stella to a rare, indulgent look of praise— "have managed to increase my guest list. And don't get me started on you." This she directed to her husband, who merely gazed back at her with amusement. "Now sit down so we can eat before the roast gets cold."

Everyone settled in at the table, deciding it was best not to push Evelyn any further towards the edge of sanity than she was already leaning, and waited for the meal to be brought in.

"You know," Vera hedged, shooting a nervous look in Evelyn's direction, "I might be able to pull together a few more people. How short is the guest list?"

"Oh dear, I don't know. We need to fill at least fifteen more chairs, and I'm not certain your London set would quite fit in." Rosemary could have throttled her mother, and it was a feeling she suspected would keep her company for the duration of her visit to Woolridge House.

"That's very nice of you, Vera. Isn't it, Mother?" she asked pointedly.

"Yes, yes, of course," Evelyn replied, waving a hand. "It's a lovely offer. I didn't mean anything by it."

Going completely against type, Vera bowed her head as if she might simply allow herself to be managed, but then thought better of it. "I happen to have some experience with raising funds for theater productions in the West End, and I've become quite close to some of the ladies who do the same. I assure you, they'll be far better company than Queenie Baker and her abominable companions, and they've deeper pockets besides. This is just the type of event they would find enticing. The novelty of a tea in the country where the locals are certain to amuse and delight, combined with the words *protection society* would draw them like ants to a picnic."

Unwilling to say a charitable word to Vera, Evelyn muttered something to the effect that the protection society was more than a penny gaff, but eventually sighed in defeat. "That would be lovely, dear," was all she could manage, though her mood brightened enough to allow for normal conversation to resume.

With a victorious smile, Vera turned her attention to Frederick. "How has work been going? Did you get that deal you were negotiating?" She included Cecil in the question, and talk quickly shifted to business.

"We certainly did," Cecil replied, "thanks to Freddie here. He really rose to the occasion. Isn't that a boon, Evelyn?"

When she didn't answer but simply stared through her husband as if he weren't there, he huffed into his mustache and continued, "Our Frederick is going to be the making of Woolridge & Sons."

"Certainly, if he can manage to see any task through to the end." Evelyn inserted a minor jab towards the son she usually placed on a pedestal and the mood once again plummeted. She then turned her attention to Stella and talk of the new addition to the family. "We're so proud of you, dear, giving us another grandchild."

Stella, who usually resided at the bottom of the sibling totem pole, preened under her mother's praise. "Rosemary wants a girl this time," she said, "and so do Leonard and I."

"That would be lovely," Evelyn agreed. "A little girl with blond curls. Did you ask your sister about the portrait?"

"Not yet," Stella said, turning to Rosemary. "Would you be willing to let Nelly sit for you while you're here? Father would like a portrait of him for his study."

Rosemary tried to picture little Nelly sitting anywhere for more than a moment at a time and failed utterly. "I'd be honored." It was a good thing she knew her subject well, or the whole caper would turn out to be a disaster.

The meal dragged on, with Evelyn and Cecil carrying on separate conversations from their respective sides of the table while the younger set exchanged furtive glances, concerned that at any moment, another war might break out in the Woolridge family dining room.

By the time Cecil suggested after-dinner drinks in the library, Rosemary was ready for a strong one. Stella had begged off for bed, claiming fatigue, which Rosemary suspected was code for having had enough drama for one day.

"Gin, please," Rosemary said to her father, who had begun filling glasses with ice from the bar cart.

"Yes, I know, you and your brother share the same fascination with that swill," Cecil replied. "Personally, I think it smells like pine trees, which is entirely off-putting. What about you, Vera, do you concur, or do you come down on the side of youth?"

Vera laughed at the mock serious expression on Cecil's face and replied diplomatically, "I'll have whatever you're having so long as it isn't bourbon. I simply can't stomach the stuff."

"Well, you won't see any of that sitting out; I've taken to keeping my bourbon in a cupboard these days," Cecil said and then winced when his wife huffed loudly.

"Don't start in on your ridiculous theory again. I simply won't have it." She pitched her voice high, and Rosemary winced.

"What theory? You must tell me, Father, I can't stand the suspense," Rosemary implored.

"Your father," Evelyn replied, not giving him the chance, "thinks someone from the society is systematically pilfering his bourbon during our meetings. It's utterly preposterous."

"Now we've got us a right mystery." Frederick ignored the furious look his mother aimed at him. "Tell us about the suspects. I'm certain our Rosie will ferret out the guilty party in no time."

While Evelyn built up anger like steam in a kettle, Cecil happily complied.

"I believe I have narrowed the culprit down to one of the young ones who come all of a piece. You won't see one without the rest."

Rosemary and Vera exchanged a look, and a smirk that Evelyn noticed and did not appreciate.

"I shouldn't think it would be the one they all look to, as she can well afford to buy her own booze. Quite well favored in her aunt's will, that one. To the exclusion of some of the cousins who might have had a bit more coming if they'd had the foresight to put in some time with the old gal. You know, rally round her feet at the final moments."

"Honestly, Cecil, that's beyond the pale."

Evelyn practically flounced up the stairs without saying goodnight, leaving those behind to sigh with relief. "Come on, Rosie, we must rally," Frederick said, pulling her along. "The she-beast is gone; we can finally relax."

Rosemary tried to hold back a smile while her father prepared cigars for himself and Frederick.

"Pay no attention to your mother," Cecil said

matter-of-factly. "She's simply overextended herself with this damnable society fête. She'll settle once it's over, and things will go back to normal." He appeared as though he needed to believe that, so nobody said a word and instead the subject was changed.

CHAPTER FIVE

The next afternoon, with the society fête being scheduled for the following day, Rosemary and Vera prepared for their trip into the village. "It's not fair!" Stella moaned when her mother insisted she stay behind and supervise the arranging of the new centerpieces.

"You sound just like you did when we were children," Rosemary teased lightly. "You could simply say no. You're a grown woman, you know."

Stella harrumphed and rolled her eyes. "No, it's fine. I rather like my place at the top of Mother's nice list. She's usually so hard on me, but now that she's angry with the two of you, I'm getting the special treatment for once."

It was true. Evelyn had always been harder on Stella than on Rosemary or her brother, though none of them were quite certain why. When Stella married an Oxford professor, she thought it a mark of good fortune, something for Evelyn to be proud of. It seemed that wasn't the case, at least until now.

"I'm perfectly happy to allow you to bask in the light of Mother's good graces as long as you can. I simply wish she wasn't being so difficult with the rest of us for hardly any reason at all. We just need to get past this event, and then, with any luck, she'll calm down."

"Ha," Stella replied. "You'd think so, but we'll just have to wait and see. Say hello to all the lovely dresses for me."

Vera raised an eyebrow. "I don't know why we're bothering; it's the village. They can't possibly have a selection similar to the shops in London. Perhaps I ought to just choose a dress from the ones I brought along."

"You might be surprised, Vera. The new dressmaker is originally from London, and she's quite enterprising," Stella explained. "She gets things from the shops there that didn't sell and makes them over to suit. If you're looking for something Evelyn-approved, that's where you'll find it."

The dress shop occupied the narrow building two doors down from the tearoom. Inside, it smelled female, of perfume and lipstick and the hope of being the prettiest woman at the party. The shopgirl wore a stylish day dress cut from a lovely printed fabric in dusky pink.

"Well, your sister wasn't wrong. There is quite a selection of ready-made things, and better cuts than I expected. Not enough frump." Vera fingered a fringed dress with a neckline far too daring to be considered appropriate for Evelyn's scrutiny. With a look of longing, she placed it back on the rack and continued to scour through the rest of the dresses.

Rosemary held a dress up near Vera's body to test the fit. "Try this one," she said. It was a lovely sheath in a demure sky blue with lace, and Vera scrunched her nose when she caught sight of it.

"All right, but I expect I'll be one shepherd's staff away from looking like Little Bo Peep." She held the garment out in front of her appraisingly while stalking around the folding screen set up for privacy when trying on.

It was the mark of a good businesswoman, Rosemary considered, to ensure her shopgirl wore fine fabrics in good cuts. Nothing like a walking advertisement for the wares.

While Vera popped herself into the dress, Rosemary perused more of the offerings, fingering the woven tweeds, smooth silks, and stitched brocades. Each color conjured a corresponding image, one she could recreate with her charcoal and paints: the flash of a crimson sail bobbing on the ocean waves, the myriad of pinks, yellows, and oranges that would bring to life a simple bowl of fruit. With her creative juices flowing, Rosemary absently picked out another dress for Vera and continued allowing the fabrics to speak to her.

"I was right, wasn't I?" Vera's voice startled Rosemary out of a daydream, and when she turned around, she had to work to hide a smirk. While the color brought out her eyes, the cut of the dress made Vera look dowdy. A feat up to now that might have been considered impossible.

"Here, try this one. Remove that horrible thing immediately," Rosemary said in response. Vera pursed her lips, and this time she veritably stomped behind the screen, her grumbles clearly audible.

It went on like that for quite some time, with Vera cycling through several possibilities she thought would appeal to Evelyn. They laughed at the flowered brocade that made Vera look as though she would blend right in with the morning room sofa, balked at a black-and-white striped pattern that made both their eyes cross, and began to get frustrated when Rosemary's favored selection ended up blending in so well with Vera's skin tone, it appeared she wasn't wearing anything at all.

"I was correct. It's hopeless. I'll just choose something out of what I brought along and hope for the best." Vera repeated her earlier lament when a fifth dress was discarded and the shopgirl's facade began to crack, irritation showing plainly on her face.

"We haven't checked those items over there." Rosemary pointed to some things hanging on a narrow rack. Something had caught her eye, and she didn't bother to listen to Vera's reply. A flash of peacock blue and violet peeked out from behind another garment, and when she pushed that one aside, Rosemary's breath left her mouth on a sigh. Tiny shimmering bugle beads stitched over the bodice formed a fleur-de-lis pattern that nipped in at the empire waistline. Below, a skirt of cerulean blue shimmered and fell like water.

Vera ran her hands along the stitching, her eyes wide. "This would be perfect for you but not for the society fête I'm afraid. This is a dress that requires champagne, and good music, and a man who looks longingly into your eyes. This is a dress made for romance, and you must try it on."

The implications were not lost on either woman, and Vera waited breathlessly to see if her friend would take that step.

"I just might," Rosemary said, lifting the hanger off

the rack and examining the dress from every angle. The shade of the skirt perfectly matched the color she'd been trying to reproduce on her canvas—the one that reminded her of the ocean off the coast of Cyprus. "Vera, dear, why don't you try on that fringed number you saw when we came in. The one with not enough frump. Just for fun."

"I will if you will," Vera said with a grin, and made a dive for the changing area ahead of Rosemary.

"Come, you can change back here." The shopgirl led Rosemary to a small area partitioned off by curtains, where fabric and trims piled around a sewing machine.

Other than the skirt being slightly too long, the dress fit like it had been made only for her, and Rosemary knew she had to have it. Rejoining Vera in front of the mirror, Rosemary gave Vera a nudge with her shoulder.

"Andrew always said you should go with the first thing that catches your eye."

"All right, you've convinced me," Vera said. "But I'll only buy it if you buy that one."

"Deal."

The loud clearing of a throat followed by the sounds of tittering cut through the jovial mood. When Rosemary and Vera spun to inspect the source, they found themselves face-to-face with Queenie Baker.

"Do they not have dresses in the big city anymore, or did you merely arrive unprepared for the fête?" she snickered. Her friends echoed the sound, but hung back slightly and allowed Queenie to serve the insults.

A fleeting, uncharitable thought that perhaps none of the rest possessed the requisite intelligence to come up with a barb of their own—not that Queenie's had been terribly original to begin with—flashed across Rosemary's mind.

"No, we simply realized the dress code leaned towards 'old lady,' and all of our clothes are far too stylish," Vera shot back.

Queenie's eyes narrowed, and her cronies quieted down a notch. "You can't possibly be planning on wearing *those*, can you?" She cast a scornful look at the dresses Rosemary and Vera had been so excited about only moments before, and while Minnie, Franny, and Olive mimicked their leader's scornful expression, Rosemary was certain she saw a flash of wistfulness on Elsie's face.

"We wouldn't dream of wearing such gorgeous dresses to a little country garden fête, Queenie," Rosemary said, her eyes innocent but her tone cutting. "We'll save these for a really spectacular evening in London."

With the raise of one eyebrow, Queenie turned just as mean as Rosemary remembered. "Well, there's no accounting for taste. If looking like cheap streetwalkers was your goal, you've succeeded."

The tittering continued, and Rosemary resisted the urge to slap Queenie across her smug face. She couldn't guarantee Vera wouldn't strike, though—she'd done it before, and Rosemary doubted it would be the last time—so she tried to diffuse the situation with a quelling look at her friend. "Come on, Vera, she's not worth it. We'll see you at the fête, Queenie. That is, if someone hasn't spiked your tea with arsenic before then."

Queenie opened her mouth to retort, but Rosemary had already taken Vera by the arm and led her back behind the screen. When they emerged a few moments later dressed in their own clothes, Queenie and her friends were gone.

"I think they must have seen us through the window; they certainly didn't spend any time shopping," Rosemary noted.

"Well, your threat probably made her think twice about sticking around."

"It wasn't a threat, just a statement of warning. If she keeps speaking to people like that, someday Miss Queen Bee is going to get what's coming to her," Rosemary declared. "And while I'd thoroughly enjoy being the one to deliver it, I'd never stoop that low."

Unfortunately, Queenie's interruption had spoiled the mood, and, having decided not to buy the beautiful dresses after all, Rosemary and Vera headed for the exit. Before they could open the door, the shopgirl emerged from the back of the store carrying a garment draped in white cloth and motioned to Rosemary and Vera.

"I found this," she said, "in the back. I think it might be exactly what you're looking for, and furthermore, it's from a brand-new pattern our dressmaker found and wanted to try. Those dreadful women haven't even seen this style yet, and there won't be another made until after your party."

Hanging the dress on a hook, the girl pulled the protective cloth away to reveal a daytime number in midnight blue with just enough glitz to satisfy Vera, but not so much as to put Evelyn off. The cut flattered Vera's curves, but wasn't overly revealing.

"It needs just a nip in under the arms." The shopgirl pulled out a piece of chalk and made a small mark. "I can have that done for you while you wait."

It was then they realized the shopgirl was actually the dressmaker. True to her word, she made the alteration in almost no time.

Practically floating on air, Vera rushed to the car and allowed the driver to carefully place the wrapped parcel in the boot of the car. While she was busy ensuring there was nothing in there that might stain, tear, or otherwise mar the prized dress, Rosemary peered down the block, noting for the first time that the dressmaker's wasn't the only new shop in the village. Rows of shoes lined one window, another carried a fine selection of stationery, and a third was filled with art supplies. It was that one that beckoned to Rosemary, but she stopped short when, just inside the stationery store window, she caught a glimpse of Queenie.

What she saw brought an uncharitable smile to her face—an outright smirk, in fact. Queenie looked up just in time to see it, and her face paled then turned a bright shade of red. Rosemary shot her a narrow-eyed glare beneath a raised eyebrow, then turned and walked away.

When she returned to the car, Vera gave her a quizzical look. "What" she asked, "is so funny?"

"Oh, nothing. I just saw Queenie Baker take a generous swig from a flask she pulled from somewhere beneath her skirts. Turns out the woman is a complete lush. On the plus side, I think she'll be more polite towards us in the future."

CHAPTER SIX

The day of the fête, preparations began before dawn, and it wasn't too long after the sun popped over the horizon when what sounded like a whirlwind of activity below permeated Rosemary's sleep.

She woke to find Vera in the act of dragging a pillow over her head to drown out the sound.

"Might as well give in to the inevitable. There will be no more sleeping today," Rosemary chided.

"Had I known your mother intended to wake up the roosters, I would have stuffed my ears with cotton wadding before I went to bed."

Frederick emerged from his room, looking slightly disheveled and more than slightly irritated, just as the ladies exited theirs in search of breakfast.

"Think we'll be able to get a bite to eat?" he asked, wrapping an arm around Vera as they all descended the stairs together.

His question was answered when they entered the dining room and found the sideboard empty, the table cleared. Cecil sat at the table, his face obscured by the folds of the morning paper, seemingly oblivious to the hubbub going on around him.

Considering he'd been receiving the silent treatment from his wife for the last several days, Rosemary wasn't surprised he'd taken on an attitude of indifference to the whole affair.

"Try the kitchen," he said without looking up.

All the boxes had been cleared out of the dining room. The windows, floors, and woodwork shone under a layer of—Rosemary sniffed the air and deduced beeswax and lemon oil from the scent of the polish. Beryl hurried out of the kitchen door before they had a chance to enter, and she was barely recognizable from the woman they had met two days before.

She wore a frock in a pale-green color that set off her eyes and made her stocky frame appear more feminine. Her hair was tucked up beneath the broad brim of a straw picture hat, which softened her angular features. Dressed for the part, Beryl was a handsome woman.

"Good morning," she said brightly. "Mrs. Shropshire's just arrived with the first load of supplies, but if you hurry you can still nab something from the breakfast trays. You'll also avoid your mother if you strike now; she's in quite a tizzy, but I'll try to keep her contained on the solarium long enough for you all to fill your bellies. You're going to need the sustenance." She winked and tottered off, ignoring the snort Cecil couldn't quite hold back.

Total chaos enveloped the kitchen, but the trio managed to find a few pieces of somewhat soggy bacon and the remains of a stack of toast. They stood back and ate, watching while the staff—some of whom were on loan from neighboring homes—rushed around in an attempt to meet the formidable Evelyn's every request.

"Mrs. Shropshire!" Rosemary exclaimed at the sight of a grey-haired old woman who was more spry than she ought to have been at her age. She received a small smile but not the kiss on the cheek or the enthusiasm with which she was usually greeted.

"Hello, loves, it's lovely to see you all, but I have to settle all these teapots. If anything gets broken, I'll be quite upset, you understand. Frederick, dear, come and lend a hand." It wasn't a demand because it didn't need to be. The number of times he'd shown up on the doorstep of her tearoom, half sloshed and searching for something to fill his belly, granted Mrs. Shropshire a certain amount of dominion over Frederick.

He nodded and said, "Anything for you, Mrs. S.," then kissed Vera's cheek and cheerfully turned his attention to the older woman's orders. "What say we set up an efficient assembly line?"

"Oh, go on with you, Freddie," Mrs. Shropshire's voice wafted back as the two left the room.

"I suppose that means we need to make for the solarium, see what we can do to help your mother. I think a soothing powder would do the trick, but we'd probably have to slip it into her tea," Vera said wryly.

Rosemary snorted—sounding quite like her father—and followed Vera out. The worst of her fears were confirmed when she saw that Queenie and her minions had already arrived and, instead of helping, were looking out the solarium windows with varying levels of interest. Rosemary stopped, placed a hand on Vera's arm, and ducked behind the doorway to eavesdrop.

"He's quite attractive, really, for a botanist," Olive said, the word *botanist* sounding like a slur. Outside the window, Mr. Murray Alden searched the hedgerows and garden borders for signs of his quarry.

Minnie giggled, the high-pitched tone making Rosemary grimace. "Maybe Franny ought to consider having a fling with him. She's desperate enough, aren't you, Franny?"

Franny's mouth opened and closed; no sound came out, but her eyes shot daggers at Minnie.

Queenie, who so far had simply gazed at Mr. Alden with veiled disinterest, took the opportunity to twist the knife a little more. "Desperate, perhaps, but she'd have to cast off her dignity and act as wanton as Elsie's nanny to turn the head of a man like that. Or have enough money to support him in style while he does his research."

In one fell swoop, Queenie managed to sink her viper fangs into two friends at the same time. Her wide-eyed gaze darting between the affected women, Olive sucked in a noisy breath and watched to see what effect the comment would have on her so-called friend. Rosemary had to agree that she couldn't imagine anyone choosing plain old Franny when the beautiful Amelia was a viable option.

Eyes firing, Franny started to say something, then just glowered at Queenie. Elsie's disapproving expression spoke for itself. Minnie looked as carefully blank as always, though dazed appeared to be her default, so Rosemary couldn't tell if she'd noticed the slight or not.

She felt Vera's body clench beside her, fists at her side, ready as always to fight for the underdog: in this case, that was Franny.

"Wait," Rosemary warned in a low, quiet tone, and felt a little of Vera's tension drain away. The gesture proved unnecessary, however, as Beryl had walked in and heard the last jab. She, proving to have less self-control than Vera or Rosemary, spoke up in Franny's defense.

"Queenie Baker, that's no way to treat your own cousin. One of these days, you're going to push someone too far and get what's coming to you. I only hope I'm fortunate enough to be there to see it. Now, why don't you ladies do something useful instead of standing around throwing barbs at one another? Elsie, come with me, I need some help in the entrance hall."

Elsie complied, appearing relieved to have been rescued from the awkward conversation.

"Wait for me," Franny said, flicking one last glance at Queenie. Rosemary couldn't tell from her angle whether it was filled with sorrow or anger, but she guessed Franny was feeling a bit of both as Queenie's smirk followed her out the door.

"Beryl is the one who will get what's coming to her," Olive spat once the three other women had exited the solarium. "These old biddies ought to realize it's time to step aside in favor of youth and vigor. Can you believe the decor in here? It looks like a jumble sale with all these different patterns and colors."

Queenie snorted while Minnie continued to stare out the window at the botanist and paid little attention to what was going on around her. Rosemary got the feeling this was a regular occurrence, as Minnie didn't appear terribly invested in the fate of the hairy spurge. It

56

seemed little had changed since their school days, when Minnie simply followed along with whatever Queenie decided, grateful to have a group of friends, no matter how nasty that group might have been.

"Evelyn has them all on her side, it's true. I only lost the chair position by one vote," Queenie replied. "Which means we need to either get one or two of them out or find some new recruits to shore up our side. I mean to take over, even if I have to keep pushing Evelyn until she hits her breaking point."

Vera hit *her* breaking point just ahead of Rosemary. It was one thing for *her* to be irritated with Evelyn, but quite another for anyone else to speak a derogatory word about her best friend and beau's mother.

"Have a care, Queenie," she said, stepping out from where she and Rosemary had been lurking. "Mrs. Woolridge has nerves of steel, and you're no match for her. I'm sorry you weren't able to bully your way into power this time and that your little cronies couldn't push you up to true Queen Bee status, but it's absolutely pathetic that you conspire to steal such a trivial honor from a middle-aged woman."

A hiccup sounded from behind Vera, and when she whirled around, it was to find that Evelyn had walked in. From the look on her face, all she'd heard was the last bit, and she refused to meet Vera's apologetic gaze.

"It's about time we all got back to work, isn't it?" Evelyn declared. "Guests will begin arriving soon, and there are finishing touches to add. Mrs. Shropshire has a plan in place for the tea service. Perhaps she needs assistance."

Queenie swallowed hard, took one look at Rosemary,

who raised an eyebrow in challenge, then shrugged and pointed to Minnie and Olive. "You two go ahead. I need a breath of fresh air."

With a smirk as though she knew that 'breath of fresh air' was a euphemism for 'a swig from my hip flask,' Minnie linked arms with Olive and followed Evelyn out.

A moment of awkward silence followed their departure, while Vera pinched the bridge of her nose as if a headache had recently formed there.

"I've done it now, haven't I?" Her tone was wistful. "I suppose I'd better go and try and patch things up with your mother," she said, and strode out of the room leaving Rosemary and Queenie alone.

Thankfully, a rustling sound caught Rosemary's attention, and the figure of little Nelly trying to sneak in through one of the windows interrupted the awkward moment.

"What on earth are you doing, little one? You're supposed to be upstairs with Nan," Rosemary chided. At the sight of the little tyke, Queenie's countenance softened.

He shrugged and said, "It's easy to sneak away during nap time. I only wait until Nan goes to sleep. I thought I might find some sweets down here." He looked at his auntie hopefully, but she shook her head.

"You don't need any sweets right now," Rosemary said. "You'll be in big trouble when Nan finds out you're not in your room."

His gaze settled on Rosemary, and for a moment, she wondered if she was off the Best Auntie Ever list for good. Then he turned his attention elsewhere.

"Hi, Mrs. Baker," he said, putting on the adorable grin

that melted hearts.

"You know I always have a little something in my bag for you." Queenie winked at him, and began pulling items from her purse as she searched. Rosemary noted that the flask did not appear, though a small velvet change purse, a gold-plated cigarette holder, and a tube of lipstick did. Finally, she fished out a handful of butterscotch candies and handed them to Nelly. "Just don't eat them all at once."

"I won't." The lie tripped off Nelly's tongue with ease, and Rosemary wondered if she ought to take the candies away. That was Stella's decision, and since she'd yet to see her sister that morning, she assumed she was busy doing their mother's bidding and decided it wasn't worth the trouble.

"Come, Nelly," Rosemary said, holding out a hand. He stuck his sticky one in hers and followed her, waving to Queenie all the way out the door.

"She's nice," he said, sucking happily on the butterscotch.

Rosemary declined to comment. Let little Nelly have his illusions now, as growing up would dispel them readily enough in time.

CHAPTER SEVEN

Rosemary deposited Nelly back in his bedroom beside a snoring Nan and watched for a few moments as his eyes drooped into sleep. Like this, he looked cherubic and adorable, and the sweet curve of his cheek tugged on her heartstrings. She closed the door quietly, on him and Nan as well as her feelings of longing. Now was not the time for melancholy. She met Vera in their room, where they changed and readied themselves and made it downstairs just in time for Vera's mother's arrival.

Lorraine Blackburn was a local celebrity, having, in her past, made a name for herself as an actress in London. Though she no longer commanded the stage, she did manage to ensure all eyes were on her whenever she entered a room. Blond hair—no grey strands to be seen—recently trimmed into a fashionable bob, and a curvy figure that defied her age made the task a negligible one.

"Evelyn, darling, everything looks marvelous!" She kissed Evelyn loudly on the cheek and then proceeded to lavish the same attention on Rosemary. "How are you keeping yourself these days?" she asked, her eyes serious despite the wide smile on her face.

"Well enough, don't you worry," Rosemary replied. She and Lorraine had always shared a special bond, and now the difference between her relationship with Vera's mother and Vera's relationship with hers was more marked than ever before.

Lorraine nodded once and whispered, "We'll talk later," to Rosemary and then moved on to Vera. "Darling, as always, you look positively ravishing! I trust you and Frederick have been enjoying your time together."

The smile that turned men's minds to mush and normally sent Evelyn into paroxysms of delight had no effect this time. Not that Lorraine noticed as she kept up her chatter. "I must thank you for always making Vera welcome in your home. Isn't it lovely, Evelyn? Just think, if your Freddie and my Vera decide to do the sensible thing, we could be in-laws soon enough!"

Evelyn made a sound somewhat like one might hear if one stepped on a duck. "I hardly think—"

Her protest fell on uninterested ears. Lorraine was lost in her own hopes and dreams. "Imagine a spring wedding, when the hyacinths are blooming. It will be the most talked about event in the history of Pardington, rest assured!"

Evelyn blanched when Lorraine clapped her hands in delight.

Meanwhile, the worker bees flanked Queenie, attempting to appear as disinterested in Mrs. Blackburn's arrival as she did. Only Minnie succeeded, though whether her indifference had anything to do with pleasing her friend, Rosemary couldn't tell. She rather thought Minnie was quite daft and wouldn't have been surprised to find that her mind was focused on something else entirely.

The other three stared, taking in every move Lorraine Blackburn made, enamored by her. It looked as though Franny wanted to say something, as she kept opening and closing her mouth, but no sound came out.

"Thank you for coming, Lorraine," Evelyn said quietly, for once not fawning all over the woman like she usually did. If there were anyone more taken by Mrs. Blackburn than Evelyn Woolridge, Rosemary had yet to meet them. This newfound coolness, she guessed, probably had something to do with Frederick and Vera's budding romance. Maybe one day, Evelyn would cut the theatrics and simply allow events to take their course rather than trying to control everything all the time.

Lorraine beamed back at her. "I wouldn't have missed it for the world," she said. "I do hope the chairs were satisfactory. Why don't you show me the solarium?"

Evelyn agreed. "Yes, I must get back to the preparations," she said, and headed for the door. Still tossing compliments like confetti, Lorraine caught up to Evelyn. She passed Queenie and her little flock of hangers-on without so much as a nod or a glance.

Before Rosemary or Vera could make a move to follow, a knock sounded on the door. Since all the staff were off doing Evelyn's bidding, Rosemary opened the door to admit a man of average face and build wearing business attire.

Practically shoving Rosemary out of the way in her haste, Queenie claimed the man's arm. "This is my husband, Abraham."

Rosemary waited a beat for the second half of the introduction and when Queenie offered none, said, "Lovely to meet you; I'm Rosemary Lillywhite, and this is my friend Vera Blackburn."

"Quite so, quite so." Abraham bobbed his head as the doorbell chimed again.

The next few minutes were taken up with greeting and assessing the parade of husbands that arrived one after the other. Each one looking barely distinguishable from the one before. Rosemary amused herself with the thought there might be a factory somewhere turning them out like life-sized dolls, each one submitted for Queenie's approval before her friends were allowed to choose. That last, though, might not have been far off the mark.

Olive and Minnie took their cues from Queenie—no shock there—and clung to their men as if worried someone might try to pry them away. Only Elsie acted like a normal human being, introducing her husband with far more decorum than the rest.

Let them play at feeling superior, Rosemary decided. Andrew would have put all four of those men to shame. With time, the pain of loss had dulled enough to allow room for the smallest twinge of pity towards the type of women who were only able to feel good about themselves when making others feel small.

"Auntie, Auntie, Auntie!" Nelly raced in the side door leading towards the kitchen, a dark-headed boy, followed by Elsie's attractive nanny, hard on his heels. He skidded to a halt in front of Rosemary. "Nigel's come to play today. Isn't that simply spiffing?"

"He's learned that from his uncle Freddie," Nan

wheezed as she caught up. "I should think you'd have been able to catch the tiny terrors." She took the younger woman to task.

"Amelia's fast, but we're faster," Nigel piped up, his little face showing no remorse for outstripping his nanny. Amelia certainly didn't look the part as she pressed a hand to her side, where Rosemary assumed, she'd developed a stitch.

When she felt Vera's finger poke her surreptitiously in the side, Rosemary's attention shifted from the children to the adults.

"Are you quite all right?" Elsie's husband, whose name Rosemary had already forgotten, stepped forward and laid a hand on Amelia's shoulder.

"Yes. It's nothing." Under his hand, the shoulder twitched, and as she was positioned to do so easily, Rosemary watched the way Elsie noticed the movement as well. The muscles around Elsie's mouth twitched, and then she turned away.

"I do apologize for letting the young ones get past me," Amelia said and hurried to round up her charges. "Come now, and if you want cream cakes for tea, you'll not run away again."

Every male eye followed Amelia the nanny's progress across the room, and when she'd gone, an uncomfortable silence descended.

With impeccable timing, Rosemary's father came to the rescue by descending the stairs. He looked quite dapper, and Rosemary's lip quirked into a half smile. Though Cecil claimed not to mind the silent treatment, he had made more of an effort on his appearance than Rosemary had seen him make in years. She wondered idly if he thought it might help him reenter his wife's good graces.

"Hello, ladies," he said, though the expression on his face indicated he'd rather walk over a bed of hot coals than be forced to navigate his way through the hairy spurge protection set.

Rosemary was expecting a third wave of new arrivals when another knock on the door came and braced herself to usher more strangers into the solarium. Instead, she discovered there was just one person waiting on the other side: Max Whittington, the one man she hadn't expected to see as she hadn't invited him.

"Why don't I show you all to your seats," Cecil said, forcing Queenie, her husband, and the rest of the couples to comply despite the blatant curiosity that showed on the women's faces when they noted Rosemary's reaction to the handsome CID detective.

"Yes, do let us join the festivities," Vera agreed, her eyes twinkling. Before she left, she crossed to give Max a welcoming kiss on the cheek, being careful not to leave a smear of lipstick, and ignoring the look of disgust Queenie didn't bother to hide.

Cecil nodded to Max and then winked at Rosemary as he turned and deftly steered the protection society members and their husbands towards the solarium. This left Rosemary alone with Max for the first time since she had put a halt to whatever romantic notion might have been between them.

"Hello, Max," she said softly. "How have you been?"

He stared at her for a long moment, stifled a sigh, and clasped her hands in his. It was a friendly gesture, with no expectation of more, and it made her heart slow back down to its normal rhythm. He gave her hands a squeeze, then let go. "I've missed our conversations," he said simply. "I've missed you."

"I've missed you, too, Max," she said, and opened her mouth to say more but was interrupted when her mother bowled through the dining room door and into the entrance hall.

Evelyn started when she laid eyes on Max but greeted him politely. "Oh, hello, Inspector Whittington." Rude wasn't her style, at least not when it came to people outside her own family. "I wasn't aware Rosemary had invited you."

"Please, call me Max. And it wasn't Rosemary who extended the invitation. It was Cecil. I thought he would have told you. I do hope I'm not crashing the party."

Evelyn waved aside his concerns. "Of course not, don't be silly. You're always welcome here." She might not care for her daughter to get involved with another law man, as she had expressed concern about Andrew's profession when Rosemary had decided to marry him.

Even though Andrew had died of a heart condition and not out in the field, there was nothing about Max, aside from his status as a detective inspector, that she could find fault with. In fact, he'd saved Rosemary's life on more than one occasion, and that granted him an appropriate amount of leniency.

Evelyn kissed Max on the cheek, much like an aging auntie, and then turned to Rosemary. "We're going to close off this door now; the guests are supposed to come in through the back entrance so they can admire the rose garden on their way past. Bertram has assigned one of the stable boys the task of routing the cars, and I'm going to lock this door."

With that, she pulled out a key, turned the lock, and then left it in place in case anyone needed to exit through the front door. Max followed Rosemary to the solarium and was intercepted by Stella almost immediately.

"Max," Stella said, "I've put you at my table along with Rosie, Fred, Vera, and Desmond. Trust me," she went on, oblivious to the sour look that crossed Max's face when she mentioned Desmond, "you don't want to be stuck with any of the old village ladies or father's boring associates."

"What about Leonard?" Rosemary asked. She'd yet to see her brother-in-law arrive.

Stella harrumphed. "He rang up earlier to say he can't get here in time. There's been some sort of cheating scandal at Oxford, and he's stuck in until it's sorted. I've become accustomed to these things, the life of a professor's wife, and would much rather be here even with Mother's hemming and hawing than at one of those tiresome formal dinners. At least, for the time being," she patted her belly and winked, seated Max, and strode off to greet more guests.

"I'll be back before tea is served," Rosemary said to Max, feeling a twinge of guilt that Frederick had arrived with Desmond in tow, but ultimately decided the men could fend for themselves.

Searching the room, Rosemary found Vera near the solarium doors.

"Both Des and Max are here, and Stella, poor soul, has put us all at the same table," she explained upon her approach. "I suppose I can't blame her; she has no idea what happened in Cyprus and assumed the arrangements would be preferable."

The debacle in Cyprus had come about during a simultaneous bid for Rosemary's affections. The two men hadn't quite come to blows, but the tension between them had been palpable for the rest of the holiday. All over a single kiss that had proved to Rosemary that despite her childhood crush on the man, Desmond wasn't for her.

Vera murmured something about everything coming to rights in the end, but her focus was on Evelyn as a new group of guests had arrived.

"Mrs. Woolridge, meet my friend Dame Penelope. Penny, this is Evelyn, who heads up the society, and the woman behind this event." If Evelyn was surprised to hear Vera refer to a knighted woman as 'Penny,' she didn't let it show. Rosemary suspected Vera had just gained a new level of respect but doubted her mother would ever admit it.

Introductions and pleasantries went on for a while, as Vera's most reputable London friends and acquaintances filled the empty chairs over which Evelyn had so greatly despaired. Finally, the deluge of guests slowed, and it was then that Vera's ultimate plan went into effect. If the attendance of Dame Penelope was a boon, the woman who arrived almost fashionably late cast that accomplishment into shadow.

"Look at Queenie's face," Vera chortled. "That shade of green clashes with her eyes, don't you think?"

Using the skills of observation she'd learned from Andrew, Rosemary watched a moment and thought none of the women in Queenie's cluster of friends seemed overjoyed. Except for Minnie, she amended, who perpetually carried a blank expression. Her husband, unlike the others who made some surface effort at attentiveness, looked even less engaged than his wife. When one of the other guests jostled his arm, it touched Minnie's, and he jerked away.

When she noticed the scrutiny, Queenie's eyes flashed hate in Vera's direction. Not bothered at all, Vera cocked an eyebrow and gave a little nod before stepping forward to greet her friend.

Lady Bainbridge accepted Vera's outstretched hands and watched with some amusement while Evelyn sank into a curtsy.

"Come on, now. We'll have none of that." Even if one were to be charitable, the Baroness wouldn't be considered an attractive woman, but below a heavy brow, her eyes were bright, and she carried smile lines around her mouth. Eager to please, Evelyn came back up so quickly she wobbled a little, then took the hand that was presented to her instead.

"Good turnout. All in service of the *Euphorbia villosa*, I hear. Nice succulent with yellow flowers. Poisonous sap, but worth preserving for borders and such. Gardening is a hobby of mine."

Rosemary recognized the adoring look on her mother's face that had previously been reserved for Lorraine Blackburn. *Mother is starstruck*, she thought with a smile.

Whether by design or accident, Dame Penelope saved the day. Coming up behind Vera, she greeted Lady Bainbridge by her given name and offered to show her the gardens.

"The roses are particularly beautiful this year," Rosemary heard her say as she led the Baroness across the solarium.

"Might I have a private word?" Evelyn's tone brooked no refusal. Rosemary and Vera followed as she weaved her way through the throng and into the corridor between the solarium and the kitchen. "Why on earth didn't anyone tell me a baroness might be coming? I would have adjusted the seating arrangements and gone with the silver tea service for that table."

Evelyn's face had gone a bright shade of crimson, and she looked as though she might begin to hyperventilate as she listed all the things she would have done differently. "And now, we're serving tea out of mismatched pots, and it's a complete disaster!"

"Please, Mrs. Woolridge, I apologize for upsetting you, but I thought you would be pleased."

"I'd be pleased if I were prepared, Vera," Evelyn snapped.

Vera closed her eyes for a half second and spoke as though she were talking to one of her actress friends just before going out on stage to begin a show. "Everything is perfect. You *are* prepared, and the place looks lovely. The Baroness is a human being, just like the rest of us, and I happen to know Mary appreciates charm more than she does elegance."

Evelyn pressed two fingers to her temples until she calmed. "All right, but I simply must do something about the place settings. She will get the Royal Albert, and that means we'll have to swap the service on Queenie's table with the ones on mine. Rosemary, can you alert the kitchen staff, please?"

"Of course, Mother." Rosemary watched Evelyn square her shoulders before reentering the solarium.

"I can't seem to do anything right, can I?" Vera lamented after she'd gone.

Her patience waning, Rosemary snapped, "If you hadn't called in your friends, this place would be a ghost town. Don't let her get to you; she holds the nobility, no matter how minor, in the highest regard. You might as well have invited the Queen, as far as she's concerned. Go and circulate and be your charming self. I'll take care of the infernal place settings."

Without waiting for Vera to answer, Rosemary turned and stalked off towards the kitchen.

CHAPTER EIGHT

Rosemary explained the debacle to Mrs. Shropshire and Beryl, who had yet to leave the kitchen and were unaware the Baroness had even arrived.

"You there," Beryl addressed one of the staff, a young girl Rosemary didn't recognize. Probably on loan from Mrs. Blackburn or the Bartons. "Come with me." Orders were given as they walked and as Beryl prepared to make the transition from behind-the-scenes helper to society member and guest.

Finally settled in her seat, Rosemary tossed a smile in Max's direction and watched as Evelyn, calmer now, cleared her throat several times and addressed the room.

"Thank you all for coming here today to support the Society for the Protection of Euphorbia Villosa. A portion of the funds raised here today will go to support Mr. Murray Alden in his noble search. The rest will be used for our village square revitalization project."

While her mother explained why that was so important, Rosemary took the opportunity to gaze around the room. She noted that Beryl and Mrs. Shropshire had made quick work of the requested changes and were on hand for Evelyn's introductory speech. Only neither woman was paying any more attention to the speech than Rosemary was. Instead, they had their heads together watching Queenie's table. Whatever the she-devil and her friends were doing, the two older women were unimpressed.

Rosemary turned her attention in that direction and felt her blood start to boil. There sat several grown women acting like children at play. Not the adorable kind like little Nelly, but the absolutely vicious types who couldn't resist making fun of others. In this case, Evelyn was the butt of the joke.

Covering her mouth with a cupped hand, Queenie leaned sideways and whispered something to Olive, who tried unsuccessfully to suppress an evil grin, then passed the message along to Minnie. Minnie smiled a bit less blatantly than Olive had, and Franny rolled her eyes but whispered to Elsie, who merely appeared disgusted at the other women's antics.

A blue china service with piping hot tea, plates of finger sandwiches, cakes, scones, and colorful macarons were quietly placed on the table, stealing Rosemary's attention. Glancing around the room, she watched the waiters perform an intricate serving dance, weaving silently between the guests as though they were on stage at a ballet, so as not to draw the attention from Evelyn.

"After tea, you will all get a chance to cast a sealed bid for some special items up for auction," Evelyn was saying when Rosemary dragged her attention back.

"Among the top items are a weekend holiday at the Pardington Village Inn, a magnum of champagne, tickets to the opera, and best of all, the necklace worn by the incomparable Lorraine Blackburn during her performance of Lady Carlton in *Secrets*, along with a signed photograph of the actress herself!"

A rumble of excitement rippled through the assembled guests, and Evelyn had to raise her voice to say, "Now, everyone, have a wonderful time, enjoy the tea and the excellent company, and later we'll embark upon a tour of the gardens." She raised her glass in a toast, flushed with pleasure when she received a round of applause, and went to sit with her friends.

"Hey, Rosie, how much do you think I should bid on that weekend at the inn?" Frederick asked with a jab of his elbow to her ribs.

"Why, Freddie, if you're planning on spending a couple of torrid nights with Vera, why not go into London and stay at a more upscale hotel like the Savoy?" she shot back.

He laughed, the untamed golden curl in the middle of his forehead bobbing into his eyes. He pushed it back in a familiar gesture and wiggled his eyebrows at Vera. "Because we don't need opulent surroundings to have a smashing time."

"You're a dog, Freddie," Vera replied, but there was no sting to her words.

"It's nice to see you two haven't gone so soft you can't poke fun at one another," Rosemary said.

Desmond leaned forward in his chair and commented, "Humor is the basis of any healthy relationship. Keep giving him hell, Vera."

"Hey, now, let's not everyone gang up on me." Frederick raised his hands in mock surrender. "If you'll excuse me, I need another drink. That last one was gone before Mother finished saying 'thank you for coming.'"

Rosemary considered reminding him that this was an afternoon tea and he had a full pot in front of him, but he would have just retorted that somewhere in the world, people were drinking gin, and therefore, it was completely acceptable for him to also partake. Since he wasn't the only one with a highball glass next to his tea, and the man behind the makeshift bar Evelyn had commissioned to be set up in the corner shook, stirred, and mixed with a fervor, she let the subject drop.

"Get me a brandy, please," she said as he rose from the table, "I might need the fortification for when I decide to put Queenie Baker in her place. Did you see how they all snickered through Mother's entire speech?" This she asked of Vera, but it was Stella who answered.

"I most certainly did," she said with a grimace. "It's probably due to the fact Queenie was well and truly sozzled before the last guest arrived. She didn't help with the preparations at all, as far as I could tell, so perhaps instead, she spent that time raiding the bar cart."

Vera snorted and exchanged a conspiratorial look with Rosemary. "Perhaps she found the bourbon cupboard."

"Who is it you ladies are discussing?" Max asked, having lost himself in the conversation.

Rosemary tipped her head in the direction of Queenie's table. "Queenie Baker, the sour-looking one in the plum-colored frock at that table over there."

Max searched the table Rosemary had indicated and shook his head. "Well, she's not there now."

"Probably off torturing the villagers," Vera replied. "It's a little brighter in here without her, I dare say."

"A little brighter without whom?" came a voice from

behind Rosemary. Teddy Barton grinned and sat down in the empty seat next to Stella.

"Queenie Baker," Rosemary stated, giving no further information, as none was necessary.

Teddy shook Max's hand and said, "Hello, Inspector. Didn't expect to see you here."

Max kept his polite face on, but his eyes flicked between the newcomer and Rosemary with veiled suspicion.

Teddy continued, either not noticing or not acknowledging Max's appraisal. "She's a pill, that one. And a lush. I saw her drain that flask she carries on her way out to the gardens. How she believes her tippling is still a secret, I couldn't dare guess. So, how long are you ladies staying on here in our sleepy little village?"

Talk switched to more mundane matters, and the group chatted away while guests finished their tea and those who hadn't submitted bids for the auction took the time to do so. A pleasant half hour passed until something caught Teddy's eye across the room. "I believe I spy the fascinating Bernadette Kingsley over there; I think I'll go and say hello."

"Go get her, Ted," Frederick tossed after him with a wink.

Teddy turned and flashed a devilish grin, then rose and sauntered towards an attractive brunette on the other side of the room. Max relaxed, and, in fact, wore a pleased smile knowing Teddy's sights were set elsewhere.

Evelyn moved to the front of the room again and motioned for people to quiet down. "We're ready to announce the winners of the silent auction, so everyone please take a seat."

Before she could exhale another breath, a loud, shrill scream erupted from somewhere outside. Max came to attention, and while everyone else simply stared dumbly at the windows, he sprang from his seat and strode towards the sound. The woman, whoever it was, continued to shriek, and Max indicated that the guests should stay put.

Rosemary looked around, and when her eyes fell on Queenie's table, her stomach began to churn. Neither Queenie nor Olive were anywhere to be seen, and dread curled in her stomach.

Before Max could make it to the window, Olive came rushing inside, still screaming at the top of her lungs. "It's Queenie! Oh, Queenie, how could this happen?"

"What has happened?" someone said.

"Queenie is dead!" Olive stumbled, and it looked like she might fall in a dead faint on the floor before getting hold of herself.

Queenie's husband went white. "Why would you say such horrible things? That can't possibly be true. Queenie is fine; she simply went outside to have a smoke."

"She's dead!" Olive continued to wail until Abraham Baker rose and slapped her soundly across the face.

"Get a hold of yourself, woman! My wife is not dead," he said, his voice quivering.

Max stepped between the two and said quietly, "I think I'd better go and see for myself. Please, sit back down."

"Who are you to make such decisions?" Mr. Baker barked back, stress turning his words to acid.

Quietly, but with great authority, Max replied, "Sir, I'm Detective Inspector Whittington. I'm more than qualified to handle the situation."

"I'm coming with you," Mr. Baker insisted, his voice raising to a boom.

With a shrug of acquiescence, Max crossed to the window, Mr. Baker and Olive in tow. Rosemary followed, as did Frederick, Evelyn, and Cecil.

"Where is she?" Max asked Olive, who led the way down the rose-lined walkway and around a corner where a small stone bench sat beneath the branches of a Japanese maple tree.

There, sprawled in the middle of the path, was Queenie, and she was most assuredly dead. Max bent to check for a pulse, even though he knew the gesture was futile. Abraham pushed him aside, then bent to shake his wife and call her name.

"Here now, she's only overcome from the drink," he said. "It was a warm day; she probably forgot herself and took a little too much."

But anyone with eyes could see Queenie's chest wasn't moving, and when that knowledge became apparent to Abraham, his expression of disbelief turned to one of horror. Next to the body were strewn the contents of her purse, which appeared to have fallen off the bench along with Queenie.

"Oh, my Queenie," he wailed. "Why?" It took some moments before Abraham could pull himself together, and even then, his eyes were glassy with shock.

"There's no wound, no blood. Did your wife have any sort of heart condition or any other problems that might have caused this?" Max asked.

Mr. Baker stared into space and muttered, "She's on some medication, yes, but her doctor has insisted she's doing quite well with it. Perhaps she drinks—drank—a little more than what I find necessary, but you know Queenie has—had—her demons."

"Don't touch anything else until the medical examiner gets here, just to be safe. Mrs. Woolridge, why don't you take Olive back inside and call the police. Mr. Baker, too, unless he wants to stay."

"No, no I don't think I can look at her like this any longer," Queenie's husband replied. He swallowed hard, allowed himself one last look, and then followed the women back down the path.

Once he was gone, Max proceeded to conduct a more thorough investigation of the body. He turned Queenie's face and pointed to what might have been mistaken for a bit of spittle at the corner of her mouth. "I believe we have another murder on our hands. I expect it's of little comfort, but at least you didn't discover the body this time, Rosemary."

CHAPTER NINE

Rosemary left Max, her father, and Frederick with Queenie's body, and her stomach flipped over at the thought of explaining the situation to a room full of party guests. She whispered instructions in her mother's ear, watched as Evelyn's face turned even more impossibly pale than it already was, and went to find Vera.

"What's happened? Is she really … dead?" Vera asked, but Rosemary simply nodded toward the front of the room where her mother had just asked for the guests' attention.

"I'm very sorry to announce," Evelyn began, a tremor to her voice, "that there's been an accident. Queenie Baker has been found, dead, in the garden." She had to raise her voice above the din as the guests reacted with gasps and exclamations. "I realize we were to announce the winners of the raffle; however, under the circumstances, it seems in quite poor taste to do so now. Someone will come around and hand out the prizes, and I'm afraid you'll all have to wait to be questioned by the police."

The statement was met with some protest, but the majority of the crowd seemed to understand that procedures must be followed. "The wait staff will be around to take drink orders and bring more tea; please try to be patient. We do appreciate all of your kind, generous donations, despite this tragic turn of events."

"Should we turn on the music, or would that be rather too macabre?" Vera asked Rosemary once the only sound that could be heard was the murmuring of the crowd.

"I don't know how it could get any more so, but I think we'd better not. Look, Mother is heading back out to the garden. Let's go," Rosemary said and pulled Vera along with her.

Upon their return to the scene of the crime, the women discovered that the police had, indeed, arrived and were examining the body.

"You were right, as usual, Whittington," said the chief inspector. Rosemary recognized the pin on his lapel and deduced that he was the one in charge. "Poison, I'd bet my life on it." The man appeared positively jovial. "Question is, who hated this woman enough to go through the trouble? Had to have been planned ahead. All sorts of suspects and witnesses. Tea, you said they were serving? Most likely method of delivery, the teacup. We'll have to take that in as evidence. Unfortunately, my good man, I'm headed out for holiday tomorrow. Any interest in taking on a temporary post and handling the case?" How the man got so many words out without appearing to take a breath between, Rosemary would never know.

She held back a snort as she came to understand the

inspector's mood. He wanted to dump the case on Max and wash his hands of it. She couldn't blame him, and furthermore, with Max in charge, she'd have a bit more control over the direction of inquiry.

"Inspector Rousseau, this is Rosemary Lillywhite" Max introduced her, and she was treated to an appraising look.

Inspector Rousseau tipped his hat as if remembering his manners and said, "So this is Mrs. Lillywhite, in the flesh. I've heard about you, and your involvement with solving the murder at Barton Manor. It's a pleasure." He shook Rosemary's hand but continued to watch her with great interest. Since most of the constabulary had resented her presence in the past, she wasn't certain what to think of him.

"Likewise," Rosemary replied, deciding not to concern herself too heavily with his opinion, despite his seeming open-mindedness regarding a lady detective, since he had already stated his intention to assign the case to Max.

Her mistrust of the man's motives intensified when he continued, "Poison is a woman's weapon, eh? Should make things easier having a female brain working on the problem." Rousseau's florid face seemed far too cheerful for the matter at hand.

"How long must we keep the guests from leaving? It's rather unsavory, having a murder take place during a fête, and I shouldn't think it will be long before they begin asking to be released. Also, you should know Lady Bainbridge is in attendance."

The inspector didn't indicate surprise or concern at hearing the name of a baroness and merely shrugged. "I see no reason to keep these people tied up. I'll station a man at the door to take statements and search handbags and pockets, but I suspect whoever poisoned her has disposed of the evidence. We'll have the premises cleared and your guests out of here as soon as possible."

Not seeming inclined to stick in any one place, Rousseau left the body and headed back towards the solarium, where anxious faces peered through the glass. Leaving Max behind, Rosemary followed to see what the inspector might do next. When he made his way to one of the tables and selected a treat from the plate in the center, she wasn't entirely surprised.

"Psst." Beryl came up behind Rosemary and drew her attention to where her mother and Mrs. Shropshire waited near one corner. "We're dying to know what's going on." She took Rosemary's arm and practically dragged her away. "Did Queenie Baker really get murdered?"

"It appears so," Rosemary confirmed. "Poisoned."

"Poison?" Olive popped out from behind a tall potted plant, her eyes wild and her face a mask of anger.

A chill passed over Rosemary, and she realized that perhaps she'd underestimated Olive after all.

"It was *you*!" Olive screamed, pointing a finger at Beryl. Minnie watched the exchange with avid interest, the ghost of a smirk on her face. Franny and Elsie only looked shocked. "You said she'd get what was coming to her, and now she's dead! You always hated Queenie. You hoped this would happen. You wished it upon her!"

"You would be wise," Beryl ground out from between clenched teeth, "to keep a civil tongue in your head."

"Or what?" Olive squawked again. "What will you

do? Kill me, too?" She formed her hands into claws and launched herself towards Beryl with the clear intention of scratching the woman's eyes out if she could.

Before Rosemary had time to react, a body brushed past her, and Frederick put himself between the two women. "You'll want a quiet spot to collect yourself, Olive. Let me just escort you to your husband." Firmly taking her arm, he did just that.

It didn't help that Beryl stared menacingly at Olive the entire time she was being put in her husband's custody, or that she gave Franny and the rest the same treatment.

A whirl of activity followed, with Rousseau and his men speaking with each guest, and Max cornered in to question first Abraham, then Olive.

Two hours later, Evelyn appeared more haggard than Rosemary had ever seen her, though it seemed she and Cecil had made up, because he hovered near her and every so often touched a hand to her elbow or waist in a protective gesture.

"Well, that's one crisis averted," Rosemary murmured to Vera. "She's allowing him within five feet of her, so all must be forgiven."

"Mmm," Vera replied, "your father is difficult to resist."

"Yes, well, she manages quite well when she's angry enough. I suppose we ought to go and assist with seeing to the guests."

Vera agreed. "I really should say goodbye to Lady Bainbridge and Penny."

After several minutes of fruitless searching, she found

both women cozied up with Evelyn, who appeared flustered in a pleased sort of way despite the circumstances.

"Mrs. Woolridge, I can't tell you the last fête I attended that turned out as interesting as this one," Lady Bainbridge was saying as they approached.

Evelyn tut-tutted. "Please, Lady Bainbridge, call me Evelyn."

"Very well. Ah, Vera, there you are, dear. We didn't get a chance to speak, though I had a lovely chat with your mother. Do come and have tea with me soon, and bring your friend. I hear she's quite the detective. You must be so proud, Evelyn. Please feel free to come as well. I can't quite promise my tea will live up to this one, but I'll see what I can do." She winked, linked arms with Dame Penelope, and glided out of the solarium.

After that, it only took a short time for Woolridge House to clear out—including Mrs. Blackburn, who reminded Evelyn to take care of her daughter, as Vera refused to leave even at her mother's urging. Unfortunately for the people who actually lived there, the wait wasn't over. Frederick, having spent most of the time since the discovery of the body tending to practical matters—likely in an attempt to get back in his mother's good graces—suggested a diversion while the police and Max finished questioning the last of the society members.

"Why don't we all retire to the parlor for a cocktail?" he suggested. "I can't imagine I'm alone in my desire to consume a considerable amount of gin and then fall into a dreamless stupor. And where did our dear sister take off to?"

Evelyn raised an eyebrow at her son. "There's no need for Stella to endure this level of stress, not in her condition. I sent her upstairs to cuddle her baby boy and get some rest."

"Sent her forcibly," Frederick muttered when Evelyn was out of earshot. "You know Stella—she loves a scandal. I'd bet every penny in my pocket she's crept down to listen to the goings on."

Before Frederick and Cecil finished mixing the first batch of drinks, Max reappeared with Franny. Her eyes were ringed with red, her makeup was smeared, and her face was covered in dried tears; she looked the part of the grieving cousin.

"My condolences, Franny," Evelyn said, crossing the room and taking Franny's hands in hers in a motherly gesture. Franny pulled away and grimaced.

"Thank you," she said. "However, I don't deserve your sympathy. The last words Queenie and I exchanged were said in anger, and I don't think I'll ever be able to forgive myself." The woman broke into a fit of sobs, one enormous heave after another.

Max offered her a handkerchief and said gently, "I'll drive you home myself, see that you get there safely."

"Thank you," Franny repeated through her tears.

"I've got to stop at the police station. There's much to be done before I sleep, but you all should get some rest. I'll return in the morning." He nodded once at Rosemary, gave her a long look, and when satisfied that she wasn't suffering any ill effects, ushered Franny out the door.

Frederick took a seat once the sound of Max's car had retreated down the driveway and crossed his legs. "Isn't that interesting," he mused.

"Isn't *what* interesting, Frederick?" his mother snapped. "I don't have the patience for any of your guessing games, given the circumstances."

He ignored the comment and, if anything, his grin widened. "Weren't we having a discussion just the other evening regarding the large sum of money Queenie inherited at the expense of the rest of her cousins? Which one of them do you suppose she left the cash to?"

"I should think her husband would inherit the bulk, but it's possible Franny will stand to gain as well," Rosemary said. "I expect we shall soon know."

Vera nodded in agreement. "Now that we have an in on the investigation. Isn't it fortuitous that Max happened to be here today?"

"Fortuitous!" Evelyn spat the word. "I suppose, then, that you would also say it was fortuitous that both a baroness and a dame were here to witness this … this debacle!"

"Mother, you must stop twisting everything into another reason to strike out at Vera." Frederick spoke in a sharper tone than Rosemary had ever heard him use with his mother. "How could she possibly have foreseen what happened here today?"

"No, Freddie, don't." Vera bit her lip and swallowed a tart retort, showing far more restraint than Rosemary had ever seen her employ. "Again, Mrs. Woolridge, I apologize. I thought having such illustrious guests would be a coup."

"And it might well have been if not for this. Not to mention what it's going to do to the society ladies. We were split down the middle before. Queenie and her bunch on one side and me on the other with Beryl and the rest. I can't imagine what will happen now, and I suspect it will be an exercise in futility to expect Beryl to ever be in the same room as Olive again."

Something about the statement niggled at Rosemary, but she couldn't put her finger on what. When her eyes wanted to cross, she realized just how taxing the day had been, and now that the adrenaline had left her system, she was positively exhausted.

"I've never seen Olive behave like that before. In school, she was a timid mouse of a girl. I didn't even know she was capable of such intense emotion as she exhibited over Queenie's death. It does beg the question of why, doesn't it? Could she and Queenie really have been that close? Or is she hiding something?"

"Obviously, someone is hiding something," Cecil said. It was the first time he'd spoken or inserted himself into the conversation, and even though his statement wasn't particularly enlightening, his words stuck with Rosemary for the rest of the evening, repeating over and over until she finally fell into a restless slumber.

CHAPTER TEN

Breakfast at Woolridge House the next morning was a somber affair. None of the family appeared to have slept well, and most showed up to the table with red rings around their eyes and frowns on their faces. Frederick was the only exception.

"How can you possibly look so refreshed?" Vera grumbled at him from beneath hooded lids.

He shrugged and sipped his cup of Turkish coffee with pleasure.

"Frederick has always been a good sleeper, even as a baby." Evelyn jumped to Frederick's defense even though she'd treated him with icy indifference for days. Rosemary guessed some habits died hard, as their mother had always given him more leeway than the rest. "I'd put him down, and within seconds he was snoring," she continued. "Lionel was the same way, but my girls were troublesome."

Evelyn's mention of Lionel drained all the color from Vera's face, and she snapped her mouth closed. Whether it was intentional or not, Rosemary couldn't say for certain, but the infrequency with which Evelyn brought up her deceased son's name made her think it was possible. She ground her teeth to keep from saying anything tart to her mother but shot an apologetic look in Vera's direction.

Cecil grimaced but didn't say anything, most likely in order to maintain his fragile footing where his wife was concerned, and Frederick's response was interrupted by a knocking at the door.

"Detective Inspector Whittington has arrived," Bertram announced and then made a hasty exit.

"Max, thank goodness you're here," Evelyn said, rushing over to greet him. Max flushed, pleased as she doted on him, practically forcing him into a seat and instructing the maid to bring out another plate, despite his insistence that he'd already been fed by Mrs. Shropshire at the village tearoom. "Have you learned anything useful to the investigation?"

Max eyed Desmond warily but nodded. "I spoke to Mrs. Baker's doctor; he confirms her husband's statement that she was on medication. Evidently, the woman suffered from heart palpitations and was taking digitalis. It wouldn't take much more for her to overdose. The cup she drank from is being tested for various poisons, but it will take time to get the results."

"I've been thinking about that," Rosemary said thoughtfully. "There was a last-minute change to the tea services. Queenie's table ended up with the pot and cups that were meant for Mother's table. If the poison was added to Queenie's cup before the change, then perhaps it wasn't meant for her at all."

Evelyn's eyes widened at the idea, and she sat down hard in her chair as the implications hit home. "Why would anyone want to poison me?"

"Perhaps you weren't the target. There were others at your table, correct? If this theory holds, the poison could have been meant for your friend Beryl, Mrs. Shropshire, or any of the other ladies. You were all in the way of Queenie taking control of the protection society's leadership role. It may not have mattered which of you received the tainted cup."

Max made a humming noise and then countered Rosemary's statement. "That's an interesting idea, and perhaps there is some weight to it, but it's something of a stretch to think this was a random attack. And an even bigger one that someone would kill over the politics of a volunteer group."

Evelyn's face went a little sour at what she perceived as another jab at the importance of her protection efforts. "I think it's marvelously naive of you, as a detective inspector, to believe that people always have a valid reason for killing. Murderers by nature have no regard for human life. They're unhinged. That's what we're looking for, someone without a firm grip on reality."

"She's right, you know," Rosemary said, though it made her stomach turn to have to side with Evelyn while she was still irritated with her mother.

"She may well be. In any case, we won't know until we get the results back, and my investigation must be predicated upon the notion that Mrs. Baker was the intended victim until I find hard evidence that she wasn't. We'll put that theory on the back burner, though I do admire your ingenuity, Rosemary, and respect your opinion, Evelyn." Max deftly dodged what could have become a row. "Now, what can you tell me about the other members of your organization? Anyone with a grudge against Mrs. Baker?"

Evelyn's mouth pressed into a thin line. "Just about everyone who wasn't in her inner circle had a grudge against Queenie, and even those women got the full treatment from her. She wasn't nice to anyone, not even her own cousin. How she ever managed to get her aunt to leave her all that money is beyond me. Perhaps the woman was also as mean as a snake."

"Money?" Max asked. "What money?"

"Queenie received a large inheritance from her aunt a few years back," Rosemary explained.

"And Franny got nothing," Evelyn elaborated. "Even though her position in the family would have indicated the sum ought to have been split between them. Queenie made it a point to mention, at every opportunity, that Franny would never see a dime, as she planned to will the money to her husband instead."

Cecil, who had yet to speak, finally did. "*That* is a valid motive for murder, if you want my opinion."

"Could we dispense with the murder talk until after Nelly has breakfast?" The question came from Stella, who had entered the room with the little guy dancing around her skirts.

"Why don't I take him with me," Desmond suggested. "We'll go and eat out by the pond, and I'll see if I can break my rock skipping record. What do you say, Nelly?"

The smile on the boy's face answered the question without a doubt, but he yelled, "Hurrah!" anyway, and allowed Desmond to take his hand.

"That would be lovely," Stella said. "I'm starved, and

someone needs to keep him out of trouble. Poor Nan found him hiding in the upstairs broom cupboard this morning. He'd taken everything out of it and was using a broom handle to whack at the back panel."

"I was *looking* for the secret package," Nelly explained.

"It's *passage*, dear, and there are none in the house, so you need to stop looking. Now, behave for Des, or he'll be forced to punish you severely."

"What's se—severely mean?"

"It means hard and without mercy, so let's just say you don't try and find out."

Nelly looked at Desmond with the eyes of a trusting child. "I'm not afraid of you. You're too nice."

"Well, young fellow, that's because you haven't managed to get on my bad side yet." Desmond winked, and Nelly grinned, and then they left through the kitchen.

Once they were gone, the conversation returned to murder. "Mr. Baker appeared distraught when he saw his wife's body," Rosemary said thoughtfully, "but, of course, that could have been an act."

"I'd bet more on one of Queenie's little minions having bumped her off," Frederick mused. "After all, poison is a woman's weapon." Vera glared daggers at him across the table. "What? It's true, isn't it Max?"

Max nodded slowly with an apologetic smile aimed at Vera. "I'm afraid that's usually the case, but there are exceptions. If the teacup comes back tainted, I'd assume a woman did the deed, but only due to the fact that most anyone who had access to that cup was female."

"What if it wasn't in the cup?" Rosemary asked

suddenly. "Queenie carried a flask around with her. I saw her take a swig from it when Vera and I were in the village the other day. She caught me watching her, and she wasn't happy that I'd discovered her little secret. Her husband could have spiked the flask; he clearly realizes she had a nasty habit. The rest of her friends, I suspect, are also aware. Even Teddy Barton knew about her drinking problem."

"Everyone was aware that Queenie was a lush," Evelyn said uncharitably. "Though it's impolite to speak ill of the dead."

It seemed Cecil didn't care much for whether or not he dishonored Queenie's memory. "I guess we know for certain who has been pilfering my best bourbon, now don't we?"

"I'm not aware of any flask found amongst Mrs. Baker's things," Max explained. "I sent the rest of her personal belongings home with Miss Cole, as the husband was in no condition to handle the responsibility. He kept going on about how she'd been cheated in life and now in death, and that he feared her soul would never rest. For now, I'm at a standstill. I'll look into this flask; however, without knowing how the poison was administered, the only thing to do is dig into Mrs. Baker's personal affairs and see if there's a better motive than her being a difficult woman."

"Well," Evelyn said reluctantly, "they're all slated to attend a society meeting here tomorrow. We were to total up the donations and decide how to divvy out the funds. Perhaps Rosemary can attend. She'll be less obtrusive than the inspector, and perhaps one of them will let something slip."

It was a proposition Max found most agreeable, likely, Rosemary guessed, because it meant he wouldn't have to spend any more time with the irritating women than he possibly had to.

CHAPTER ELEVEN

Rosemary dipped her brush in a splotch of forest-green paint and applied it to her canvas with careful strokes. She peered across the pond behind Woolridge House, relishing the moment of peace. She loved working outdoors with only the smell of turpentine to keep her company. She changed brushes and switched her attention to the foreground of her painting, where she dabbed in a few boulders and the small pile of flat rocks that she suspected Nelly and Desmond had left behind the day before.

As if thinking about him had summoned him forth, she spied Desmond walking across the lawn towards her.

"That's coming along beautifully," he said, gesturing to the painting.

"I'd like to get Nelly to sit out here for me, but I doubt I can get him to settle for that long. Father wants a more traditional portrait, I expect, anyway," Rosemary replied, biting her lip as she stood back to appraise her work. She laid the brush back down and took a seat next to Desmond on the large, flat stone that had been the topic of much debate between her parents. Cecil believed the stone made a perfect spot to sit and overlook the pond, while her mother believed it detracted from the view.

"How have you been keeping?" Desmond asked. "We haven't had the opportunity to speak since I arrived and everything went to hell in a handbasket."

Rosemary wished people would stop asking her how she felt but didn't say so because she knew it came from a place of concern, and after all, there had been a murder in her backyard two days before.

"I'm fine, Des." She repeated the phrase for what felt like the millionth time.

An awkward silence followed, and Desmond finally sighed and got to the point. "I miss you, and I'm sorry if I upset you in Cyprus. However, I don't regret what I said or what I did."

As enlightened and liberated as she might consider herself, Rosemary's face still flamed when Desmond referred to the kiss they had shared. "I don't regret that moment, either; I'm simply not ready for anything more. I hope that's all right with you, because your friendship is important to me."

It was the truth, and it was the second time since arriving in Pardington that Rosemary had been forced to dash a man's hopes.

Desmond nodded and swallowed hard. "Of course," he said, always a gentleman. "I understand. Friends we will be until you decide otherwise. And you will decide otherwise, Rosemary. I have faith."

Unsure how to answer, Rosemary was relieved when she heard the crunch of tires that indicated an car was making its way up the drive. Relieved, at least, until she remembered that the SPEV women were slated to hold a meeting that afternoon.

"I suppose I ought to go and save Vera from having to deal with the vipers by herself. I'm not at all looking forward to this," Rosemary explained, tidying up her easel. "I'd better go and wash and change first, or I'll never hear the end of it." Desmond helped her carry the easel inside and assured her he would see it safely stored.

Quickly making herself presentable, Rosemary entered the solarium where Evelyn was busy getting the group settled—a difficult task under normal circumstances, and an even greater feat given the palpable tension in the room.

"Wouldn't it be better to sit out in the gardens?" Minnie whined. "It's such a beautiful day."

Evelyn ignored her, as she'd already had the space prepared for the meeting, but rolled her eyes skyward.

Mrs. Shropshire and Beryl took a seat on one side of the long rectangular table that had been set up for the meeting, leaving a space for Evelyn between them. Elsie and Minnie flanked Olive, who held her head in a haughty manner. One might deduce, Rosemary thought, that Olive had taken over Queenie's role as leader of the group. Olive glared at Beryl, as did Minnie, and Beryl glared back.

"We're here to discuss organization matters," Evelyn said above the din. "However, as I find myself quite unconcerned about the preservation of anything right now, I suggest we dispense with the guise and see if we can figure out who might have wanted Queenie dead."

It shocked Rosemary to hear her mother speak such candid words, and a rush of pride swelled inside her. She suspected Evelyn's candor had something to do with the possibility of tainted tea having been meant for her or one of her friends, but the reason mattered little. What did matter was that Evelyn was prepared to meet the situation head on instead of employing her usual method of sidestepping anything she considered unsavory.

Olive's eyes widened, and she said testily, "Isn't that a matter best left to the police?"

Evelyn stared her dead in the face and said, with pity in her voice, "One would think, wouldn't one? However, my Rosemary has solved several murders, so ignoring the fact that she might be able to sniff out the culprit before the police can would be grossly negligent. Wouldn't you all agree?"

While the older women nodded, it was the younger group of Olive and her friends who appeared reluctant. "I agree with Olive," Minnie said. "It's best to let the police inspector handle it. After all, this is men's work, isn't it?"

Vera couldn't hold back a snort. "What kind of modern women are you?" she asked, incredulous that any woman in her age bracket could be so hidebound.

Mrs. Shropshire spoke up. "I, for one, have the utmost confidence in Rosemary's abilities. You'd all do well to cooperate with her."

"I expect you do feel that way," Olive retorted, "just as I expect Evelyn's daughter won't be pointing the finger in any direction that would put a blot on the reputation of anyone in her circle. Mummy wouldn't allow it."

Back in her trousers and rough shirt, Beryl looked slightly menacing when she barked her retort. "Evelyn wouldn't stand for anything less than the truth, no matter the cost. Queenie Baker wasn't a nice person. I'm certain we can all agree on that point, but being unpleasant isn't a good enough reason for murder."

"Then what *is* a good enough reason?" For once, Minnie wasn't focused on whatever it was that went on in her head. "Losing control of the protection society? Being usurped by those with more life and energy, maybe? Or did Queenie learn your dirtiest secret? You tell me, Beryl, because you are the only person I heard casting threats in her direction, and not long before she died."

Every head turned towards Beryl, who rolled out a laugh. "I do have a dirty secret. Would you like to hear it if I promise not to kill you after?" She laughed again when Minnie's face went sour. "Here it is. I use horse manure to fertilize my courgettes."

Olive gasped and sputtered. "You gave me three courgettes last week, and we made them into soup." Her face had gone a bit green.

"Well, now you know my dirty secret, and I have no desire to murder you at all. As to threatening Queenie, I merely said she should get what was coming to her, by which I meant that someone ought to stand up to her. Something you all should have done long before it came to spiking her flask with poison."

Having said her piece, Beryl cocked an eyebrow and settled back into her seat.

"There was no flask." Olive drew herself up tall. "How dare you say such a thing about Queenie! She

100

hardly drank a drop."

Had Olive's gaze not skidded sideways, Rosemary might have believed her ignorant of the facts, but then a chorus of agreement went up among the Queenie supporters, and it looked like they'd planned to present a united front. Since she'd seen the flask with her own eyes, Rosemary decided not to pursue that line of questioning, as it would have been futile.

In fact, she decided, it might be better to poke the bees' nest and see what came out than to expect an ounce of cooperation.

"It's quite all right, Beryl. I suspect Queenie was the type to know more about others than she allowed them to know about her. Especially those whom she considered beneath her status. It's far more likely none of her friends have enough insight to be particularly useful in finding her killer."

A tremor ran through Vera, and when Rosemary slid her gaze sideways, she noted the corner of Vera's mouth twitching with humor. What Rosemary didn't need right now was a bout of the giggles, so she jabbed an elbow into her friend's ribs to forestall the possibility and watched to see whose resolve would crack first. Had there been time for a wager, she would have put her money on Olive.

Had she wagered, Rosemary would have lost.

"Queenie hid nothing from me. She said I was as close as family to her," Minnie spat. "Closer than some." She pierced Elsie with a look. "Close enough to gift me her grandmother's ruby pendant."

Elsie snorted. "You might want to get it appraised. Her grandmother's ruby pendant went down with her aunt Ida on board the Titanic in 1912. I'm quite certain what Queenie gave you was nothing more than a paste replica."

Unconvinced, Minnie argued, "Maybe she didn't know it had been replaced."

"She knew. She told me her grandmother lamented the loss of the necklace above the death of her only daughter."

Vicious women must run in that family, Rosemary thought with disgust.

Olive came out of her stupor long enough to say, "I knew. Queenie found it amusing to watch you fawn all over her as if it were real every time you wore the necklace. It's no different from her talking Elsie out of that exquisite, cream-colored wedding frock so she could go back and buy it later."

"She never." But the way Elsie chewed at her lip said she wasn't certain.

"Oh," Minnie chimed in, "yes, she did. It looked well on you, as I remember."

"Not as well as Queenie thought it would look on her." Olive let a hint of a smile play over her lips, but it didn't reach her eyes. "Though she never wore it, nor intended to. She only wanted you not to have the dress."

"That's the second-most vile thing I've ever heard," Elsie said. "You'd know the first very well, though, wouldn't you Minnie?"

At that, Minnie subsided, and a choking silence descended until Evelyn broke in.

"I think we've had quite enough talk of Queenie for one day. Shall we move on to the next order of business?"

CHAPTER TWELVE

"Come now, come now, it's time for dinner." Evelyn poked her head into the library, where a lively debate on whether a Southside was a worthy drink or simply a gimlet spoiled by orange bitters had been raging over pre-dinner cocktails. Frederick had run his fingers through his hair so many times it stood on end, and his mother peered at him with reproach. "You'd better clean yourself up before you sit down at my table," she warned before retreating to the dining room.

"I prefer mine with a twist in any case," Vera announced.

The conversation continued into the dining room, where the table was set with some of the leftover fête candlesticks, creating a lovely glow over Evelyn's favorite china. Stella and Nelly had already taken their places to the right of the head of the table, with Evelyn seated on the opposite end flanked by Desmond and Frederick.

Rosemary strode to her regular seat beside Nelly and noticed something amiss. "Mother," Rosemary said with a raised eyebrow. "We're missing a place setting. Where is Vera supposed to sit?"

Evelyn's eyes widened unconvincingly. "Why, I don't know, dear. The maid must have made a mistake," she said innocently. "I'll just go and check."

She tottered off towards the kitchen, leaving Rosemary with a sinking feeling in her stomach.

"Des, why don't you take the seat next to Rose and let Vera sit here beside me," Frederick said after casting an irritated look at his mother's back.

Several minutes—minutes that felt like an eternity—later, Evelyn returned with the maid on her heels. "I'm sorry, madam, I thought you said seven for dinner, not eight."

"It's all right, Gerta," Evelyn replied breezily. "These things happen."

And that was the clincher as far as Rosemary was concerned. Never in her life had she seen her mother pass up an opportunity to harass the staff. If Gerta had indeed misheard her, Evelyn would have seen to it that she was duly reprimanded.

With one eye on his mother, Frederick leaned over and whispered something in Vera's ear once she'd settled in next to him. Her tinkling laugh made Evelyn's jaw clench, which Rosemary supposed had been the point.

"You are such a rogue, Frederick Woolridge." Vera's tone belied the sentiment. "It's no wonder I'm stuck on you." Studiously ignoring one end of the table, she looked towards the other and said, "I think he takes after you, Cecil. He's handsome and witty."

Evelyn made a strangled sound, something between a gargle and a cough. From her vantage point, Rosemary noted Vera's answering smirk, faint though it was, and resisted the urge to rest her forehead on the table in despair. If this foolishness between her mother and her best friend wasn't resolved soon, she might give in to the temptation to lock them both in a room until it was.

When Bertram announced the arrival of Inspector Whittington, albeit with some disapproval because of what he considered impolite timing, Rosemary wasn't the only one who was thankful for the interruption.

"I'm sorry to interrupt your dinner." Max looked longingly at the platter of poached salmon sitting in the middle of the table. "But I have news about Mrs. Baker's murder."

Cecil rose from his place, tossed down his napkin, and shook Max's hand. "Nothing to worry about; why don't you sit down and have a bite to eat." With the seat next to Rosemary already occupied by Desmond—a fact that didn't go unnoticed by Max—he allowed Cecil to place him at the other end. Far faster than had happened when Vera needed a place setting, the maid hurried out with all that was needed to get Max seated and his plate comfortably filled.

Grateful, Max picked up his fork, selected a portion of flaky fish which he raised toward his lips, then noticed the expectant gazes turned his way.

"The good news is, no trace of poison was detected in the teacup. Which means that it was administered via another method. Possibly, and most likely, the flask Rosemary mentioned. Unfortunately, the flask wasn't found when we swept the property, and Mrs. Baker's cousin, Franny Cole, claims it wasn't in with her personal belongings."

"And the bad news?"

Max sighed, set his fork back down on his plate, the bite of salmon still on it, and shifted in his chair. "The bad news is that it seems Mrs. Baker left her money to Miss Cole after all."

"Which means," Rosemary deduced, "that she has a motive. Not only to kill Queenie, but to lie about the flask, if that was indeed the murder weapon."

"Doesn't it also mean Queenie was the intended target? The poison couldn't have been meant for Mrs. Woolridge, nor for any of her friends." If Evelyn couldn't hear both hope and relief, it was from willful refusal, since both were evident in Vera's tone.

"Have you considered," Stella said, "that Queenie might have taken the poison on purpose?"

"Suicide?" Scandalized, Evelyn put her fork down, pushing her plate away as if the meal had lost all appeal. "Why, that's a crime. What a hideous thing to suggest."

There, Rosemary thought, went Stella's moment in the sun of her mother's approval.

"So is murder," Frederick pointed out. "A crime, that is."

"Yes, but suicide is a crime against the church."

"Deuced hard to punish the dead, though, hey Inspector?" Cecil earned a quelling glance from his wife, and when a discussion over the degree to which suicide might outrank murder was entered by the rest of the assemblage, Max took the opportunity to finish his meal.

Not as impassioned by the conversation as the rest, Rosemary turned the possibility over in her mind. There had been, she remembered, a moment where Abraham had looked upon the still face of his wife and asked *why*. Could the question have been directed at Queenie and not on her behalf?

If that were the case, then Queenie had brought the poison with her, probably in her flask, but why would she choose such a public manner in which to end her life? And why, then, hadn't the flask been found near her body, if death would have been immediate?

Having put her theory to the table, Stella had gone silent to avoid another round of chastisement from her mother. Intending to ask what had sparked such a suggestion, Rosemary tried to catch her sister's eye, but Stella remained focused on her plate while the debate raged around her.

It ended in stalemate with Evelyn adamantly opposed to the possibility.

When dinner was over, Cecil insisted upon returning to the library for after-dinner drinks, pulling Max along with him and winking at Rosemary over his shoulder. This was the second time he had done such, leaving her no other option but to consider it some veiled attempt to convey his approval of Max as a suitor.

Would no one in her life see fit to let her handle her romantic attachments—or lack of the same—without comment, whether overt or oblique?

"Evelyn, why don't you fix us some drinks, and we'll hash this whole thing out," Cecil said, as though sitting around in armchairs and talking about it might somehow miraculously solve the case. Rosemary admired his optimism, but she had a sinking feeling that a more proactive approach was the only way to find out exactly who hated Queenie enough to follow through with removing her from the mortal coil.

Evelyn scowled as she approached the bar cart and began pulling tumblers from the bottom shelf. The spoon tinkled against glass, and after a few minutes, she pressed a glass of brandy into Cecil's hand.

"G&Ts for Frederick and Desmond; a brandy for Rosemary, and Max—would you like a bourbon or perhaps some of this rum Frederick brought with him? It smells like swill to me; however, the young ones seem to enjoy it quite well."

She absently passed a glass of amber liquid to Vera, who gingerly sniffed it and then tried to hold back a grimace. "Is this bourbon, Mrs. Woolridge?" she asked, her voice wooden.

"Why yes, of course, Vera dear. Isn't that what you drink?" Again, that innocent expression that Rosemary recognized as completely false crossed her mother's face.

The tension in the room rose a notch, and Frederick glared at his mother with barely controlled ire. "I'll trade you, Vera dear," he said in a nauseatingly mushy tone that mimicked his mother's. "You take my gin and I'll choke down your bourbon."

Desmond wisely kept quiet, which was a trait Rosemary had come to both appreciate and abhor, and Max looked at Rosemary, bewildered. He, of course, being trained to read the mood of a room, could sense the tension just as well as the rest of but but had no idea of the source.

"That would be lovely, Freddie dear," Vera replied in kind, only she expressed her term of endearment in a genuine manner, accompanying it with a gentle touch on his hand.

The sight of the woman she considered not good enough for her son looking at him with such tenderness sent Evelyn deeper into the grip of her own personal madness.

"Mother, may I have a word with you?" Rosemary had hit her limit. "In private." She eyed her mother sternly.

"I'm terribly busy right now, as you can plainly see. We have guests."

Dragging her mother bodily from the room was an option worth considering, except Vera caught Rosemary's eye and shook her head.

Frederick yawned and raised an eyebrow at Vera. "It's getting quite late," he said, though it was barely going on eight o'clock. "Why don't we take our evening constitutional around the grounds, and then I'll see to it you get to your room safely. Don't fret, Mother, we'll avoid the rear gardens, just in case Queenie's murderer has come back for a second round."

"Your idea of a joke isn't funny, Frederick," Evelyn snapped. "And you've got a full day tomorrow, so don't stay out too long." She cast a sidelong glance at Vera, but without any actual reason why her adult son ought not to roam about the property, didn't say anything else.

"That's quite a fine idea, Fred. I think I'll head on up to bed myself; leave you young ones to it," Cecil remarked with a pointed look at his wife. When she would have argued, he merely took her hand and left her no choice.

Vera, who Rosemary thought might choose to come to her aid, was next to go, with an arm around Frederick's waist. With a mischievous glint in his eye, he left his sister alone with two men keen enough to compete for her affections.

Like rats leaving a sinking ship, Rosemary thought as Frederick whistled a jaunty tune on his way out the door.

Max's face showed nothing of his thoughts at having been left with the object of his affection as well as his nemesis for said affections. In fact, rather than attempt to choose words with which to rouse Desmond, he merely sat back, lit a cigarette, sipped his bourbon, and let a direct gaze do all the work. Finally, it was Desmond who gave in to the game, and lowered his own eyes.

"I suppose you two have much to discuss. Rose, I'll see you tomorrow. I've not forgotten your promise of a horseback tour of the grounds."

Rosemary listened with a raised brow. Desmond had been coming to Woolridge House since he was a boy; she doubted there was a nook or cranny left on the property that he hadn't already explored.

"Let's say early in the morning? I'll knock on your door." He glanced at Max pointedly, as if pushing home the reminder that he was a welcome guest who enjoyed a long history with the Woolridge family.

Rosemary shook her head. "Not tomorrow morning, Des, but the day after, if that's all right with you." He appeared crestfallen but agreed and took his leave.

Once he was gone, Max visibly relaxed. He watched while Rosemary poured herself another brandy. "What exactly has been going on around here?" he asked. "The tension is positively palpable."

Rosemary flashed him a wry smile and explained. "It

seems that Mother isn't pleased that Vera and Freddie have become an item. You knew she was engaged to my eldest brother, Lionel, who was killed in the war, did you not?"

When Max nodded, she continued. "Mother wasn't thrilled with that match either. I've never understood why she's never warmed to Vera. Especially with the way she feels about Lorraine."

Max shrugged as if he found people and their actions baffling.

"Still, Mother kept her opinion to herself because Lionel wouldn't have appreciated her meddling, and whatever Lionel wanted, Lionel got. Anyway, now that Vera is with Frederick, things have been exceedingly tense, just as you surmised. It took a lot for Vera to let go of the past, and she's happy with Frederick. He's happy with her; I simply can't understand why Mother can't also be happy for them."

As Rosemary settled deeper into the corner of the settee in order to put a tiny bit more distance between herself and the man seated on the other end, she realized she might be babbling.

"None of us ever pictured Freddie as a family man, and you would think it would make her happy that he might be getting close to settling down. It's too soon to tell, of course, but my gut tells me they'll be married within a year. Unless Mother manages to ruin it for them."

Max grimaced and ran a finger around the rim of his tumbler of bourbon. "I doubt that's her real goal. Mothers always believe they know what's best for their children, and while the children never think so, it's very often true. Perhaps there's some deeper reason why she feels as she does. Vera does have something of a reputation for flitting from one man to the next."

If there had been an iota of condemnation in the observation, Max might have found himself wearing the remains of her brandy. As there wasn't, Rosemary uttered a truth that said as much about herself as it did about Vera.

"Some people cope with tragedy by burying themselves in silence, others fill the void with flash and noise. There's more to Vera than most ever realize, and my mother certainly can't see that Vera is trying hard to win her approval."

"No matter how old we get," Max said, swirling the amber liquid in his glass, "I think we desire the approval of our parents. It means more than some would like to admit, but there you go. I've seen more than one hope of marriage dashed due to a man's mother's disapproval."

"Freddie won't let Mother's wrath stop him. I think he enjoys getting her all stirred up," Rosemary mused. "I suppose that's how a man must deal with such obstacles if he wishes to win the fair maiden."

She recalled the one occasion when she'd been introduced to Max's mother, and the overwhelming feeling that the lady hadn't approved of Rosemary even though they had yet to engage in an actual conversation. It had stung—she was willing to admit that much.

Some of the tension he'd lost earlier seemed to creep back through Max's bones. He shifted more toward Rosemary and she saw his furrowed brow.

"I suppose it might seem that way to you," he said slowly, his eyes having become unfocused as though he were lost in a thought or a memory. "However, I think family harmony is often worth more than personal happiness. How solid can a relationship be if it's surrounded by discord? Furthermore, how solid if an unkind word or two is all it takes to shake it?"

"One's family ought not to interfere with true love," Rosemary insisted, indignation rising even though she couldn't quite figure out why his words had raised her hackles so.

"True love is a rarity; I'm not certain it even exists, to be perfectly honest. I think there are many people in this world whom we could love. Many people we could find happiness with. I'm simply suggesting that when there's harmony within a family, relationships have a chance to grow, unimpeded by conflict."

Rosemary, having some experience at extricating herself from unpleasant conversations, yawned exaggeratedly, and Max drained his glass before stating that he'd better call it a night.

"I'll be in touch," he said stiffly on his way out. It felt like a wall had been built between them, and she wondered if she'd get the chance to try and tear it back down. Seeing Vera, stars in her eyes, splayed across the bed in her room, did nothing to allay the feeling.

"You look far too happy," Rosemary said grumpily, plopping down on the edge of the bed.

Vera sat up straight and, being the excellent friend that she was, drew her face into a serious expression. "What's the matter, Rosie?" she asked sincerely.

"I'm feeling rather melancholy," Rosemary replied.

"Your conversation with Max didn't go well?"

Rosemary sighed and rolled over onto her stomach.

"No, I suppose it didn't." She related the pertinent points to Vera. "I suppose I'm feeling as though perhaps Max isn't as steadfast as I thought. I can understand wanting to please your family, but I would like to hope that any man who loved me would choose me over his mother. Is the idea so terribly wrong?"

As she expressed the thought, she heard how it must have sounded.

"This is because Max's mother wasn't keen on you, isn't it?" Vera always did manage to see through to the truth of a thing.

"Perhaps," Rosemary replied, her focus attuned to a loop of thread that poked out of the bedspread. "Yes, I think that's an accurate assumption. I believe it's possible that I'm in love with Max."

Vera wasn't the least bit surprised. "Well, dear, at least you've finally admitted it. We've been taking bets on when you'd figure it out. Of course, your brother still has his heart set on a match between you and Desmond, but he would never begrudge you your happiness should you decide Max is your beau," she hastened to add.

"I suppose time will tell, but I'm more concerned about what's happening between you and my mother," Rosemary lied.

"Don't you worry your pretty little head about that," Vera said with an evil grin. "If it's a war your mother wants, that's exactly what she's going to get."

CHAPTER THIRTEEN

"I want that dress, Rose," Vera said the next morning, mere moments after waking. Rosemary opened one eye and glared at her friend, grunted, and closed it again. "I can't stop thinking about it, and now it's made its way into my dreams. We were at a lovely fête in London—one where nobody turned up dead—you in that peacock-colored frock and me in the blue sheath dress. Can't we go into the village today? It will give us a chance to visit Mrs. Shropshire too."

Vera's logic was sound, and Rosemary couldn't help but agree that she'd regretted leaving the exquisitely beaded work of art behind. "I do need to pick up some supplies for the portrait I'm painting of Nelly. All right, we'll go, but not until I've had a cup of coffee and cleared the sleep out of my eyes." She rolled over and sighed, snuggling further into the blankets.

By the time Vera had finished getting dressed and ready, Rosemary had fallen back to sleep and was awoken again by her friend bouncing on the edge of the mattress. The jostling roused her, and she sat up, her hair a disheveled mess. "All right, all right, I'll get dressed," she said, unable to keep herself from smiling at Vera's childish antics. "We have to hurry, because Elsie is bringing her son over to play with Nelly, and we can't pass up the opportunity to grill her for information."

"Don't tell me we're in a hurry after you fell back to sleep!" Vera chided with a poke to Rosemary's shoulder. "You'll have to investigate on your own, Rosie; your brother has plans for me and him today. He says if he doesn't get away from your mother for a few hours—"

"Enough said," Rosemary cut in. "I'd rather not bear witness to another row between the two of them or the two of you. They don't often argue, but when they do … let's just say it's better to be far from Woolridge House."

"Then it's settled. We'll pop into the village, buy the dresses, have some tea and gossip with Mrs. S., and be back here just in time for whatever your dear brother has cooked up. Without any information, I'm at a loss for what to wear. Perhaps I'll find something at the shops …" She ran through a list of items Rosemary knew good and well she didn't need, and the quick jaunt into the village began to look like it might take far longer than originally planned.

Last night's conversation with Max felt like a dream in the harsh light of day, and though Rosemary suspected the rush of feelings had been legitimate, she was more than happy to push them into the back of her mind rather than face the repercussions of the admission.

She did just that while she dressed quickly, and the pair found themselves standing outside the village dress shop less than an hour later. Rosemary made a beeline for the rack where she'd first found the prized fringed frock and, feeling victorious, held it up to admire the beaded handiwork.

To Vera's frustration, her dress was not found quite so easily, and neither was the dressmaker. "I'll keep looking if you want to try that on again," she said, waving away Rosemary's offer to help her search.

Rosemary retreated behind the screen and was halfway out of her skirts when she heard a wet sniffling noise coming from the curtained area where the seamstress did her work. She felt like an intruder, listening to the woman sob, and hastened to finish dressing so she could leave and afford her some privacy. Her efforts were in vain, for at the very same moment Rosemary stood to walk from behind the privacy screen, the other woman appeared.

"Franny!" she said with surprise as Queenie's cousin came to a short stop in front of her.

"Hello, Rosemary," she sniffled.

Rosemary's heart went out; she couldn't help it. She understood the effects of grief better than anyone and, at that moment, would have bet money on the fact that Franny was truly in distress.

"Are you all right?" Rosemary asked, realizing even as she spoke the words just how trite they sounded.

Franny wavered, as if wondering whether she should confide in Rosemary, and finally wailed, "It's just so awful! I was so angry with her, and then—and then—it turns out she didn't hate me as much as I thought. I should have tried harder. I should have understood she didn't mean all the things she said. She had to take it out on someone, and it was me!"

"Had to take what out on someone?" Rosemary asked gently, confused.

Vera poked her head around the corner just then, no doubt summoned by Franny's hysterics. "I found it! Oh, hello, Franny. My sincerest condolences to you on the loss of your cousin."

That set Franny into another fit, and it took a concerted effort to pry the black funeral dress from her clenched fingers. Vera took the garment, along with her dress and Rosemary's, and paid for the lot while Rosemary ushered Franny out onto the pavement.

"Why don't we get you a cuppa," Rosemary suggested. Dazed, Franny nodded and followed her into Mrs. Shropshire's tearoom.

Mrs. Shropshire was busy bustling around and serving customers—if *serving customers* meant shamelessly gossiping, which, in Pardington, was exactly what it did mean. She looked up when the three women walked in, her eyes widening slightly and then narrowing when she noted Franny accompanying Rosemary and Vera.

"Why don't you all sit over here"—she waved towards a secluded table in the back of the tearoom—"and I'll bring you a pot."

"Thank you, Mrs. S.," came Rosemary's reply as she settled Franny into a chair. Franny slumped over the table and pulled a handkerchief from her handbag, blowing her nose discreetly and then clutching the scrap of cloth as though it were a lifeline.

The tea arrived a short time later, and in the interim, Franny looked at Rosemary and Vera, wide-eyed, but silent. "Why are you being so nice to me?" she finally asked while she stirred a bit of milk into her cup.

Taken aback, Rosemary and Vera exchanged a sidelong glance. The statement was more direct than they were used to from Franny, who had always faded into the background. Of course, none of her friends were there to direct the conversation, and Rosemary got the impression she was speaking with an entirely different person than the one she'd known as a child.

"We're not horrible people, you know," she said to Franny. "You're in distress, and we're not schoolgirls anymore. I don't remember *you* being central to any of the squabbles."

Franny's face scrunched into a pained expression. "I'd rather not tear my cousin to shreds, if you don't mind. She is dead, after all. Her torturing days are over."

"I'm sorry, Franny, truly. I wasn't making a jab at Queenie, merely stating a fact. I know how difficult this must be for you, and I truly am sorry she's dead."

"As am I," Vera reiterated, and then quieted, allowing Franny a moment of rumination.

She sighed, and nearly erupted into tears again, but instead took a long sip of her tea. "Queenie wasn't as bad as everyone thought," Franny said sadly. "She was simply taken over with grief. Her mother died when she was quite young, you know, and my uncle is ... well, let's just say Queenie got her mean streak from him. All Queenie ever wanted was a family of her own to love. She wanted a child more than anything, but the doctor said she was barren. It was a blow, certainly, and one from which Queenie never recovered."

Queenie's plight was one with which Rosemary could identify, if not for the same reason. There hadn't been a chance for children with Andrew, and it stung. She couldn't imagine how she'd have felt in Queenie's place, and a stab of pity for the dead woman pierced her heart.

Then she remembered how Queenie had acted in school. How she'd tormented anyone who was less fortunate than she was, how she'd set out to make everyone feel worse than she did, and the look on her face when she'd contemplated ousting Evelyn from her seat as chairwoman of the preservation society. Her heart once again hardened, though she hid it well behind a sympathetic smile for Franny.

"I know it's no excuse, truly I do, but she was family, and I don't have much left. Even less now." Franny's eyes focused on something only she could see, and she shook her head before coming back to the conversation.

"Hello, lovely ones, is there news?" Mrs. Shropshire could smell if the balance of flour to fat in short crust pastry was off, but where her nose truly shone—unless it was powdered, of course—was in sniffing out the faintest whiff of gossip. Franny at one of her tables, teary-eyed and sniffling in public meant news. "Has the killer been caught?"

"Not as yet." Rosemary shook her head. "But there has been a development in the investigation. Max, I mean Inspector Whittington, says there was no poison in the teacup. Queenie was killed by some other means."

Mrs. Shropshire huffed. "That is good news for Beryl. Not that I thought for a moment she was capable of murder, mind you. What utter madness." She might have said more if her words hadn't set off another spate of sobbing from Franny.

"It's nice to see you so happy about your friend, but

what about my cousin? What about poor dead Queenie? Doesn't anyone care about her?"

"Yes," Vera said sharply. "What about her? None of you lot seem terribly interested in helping run down her killer. Closed ranks is what your friends have done, when they could have given information that might lead to an arrest. It's your contingent who don't seem to care."

If nothing else, Vera's vehemence shut off Franny's waterworks.

"What a positively beastly thing to say, Vera Blackburn."

Vera leaned back in her chair, lifted her nose, and looked down the length of it at Franny. "Prove it," she said. "Tell us who you think is the killer."

A moment passed while Franny paused, and Rosemary allowed the hope to blossom that she might actually impart some helpful information. When she finally spoke, that hope was dashed.

"I haven't the foggiest. I thought, at first, she'd done it herself on account of not being able to become—" face flaming, Franny whispered, "in the family way." Her voice returned to normal as she continued. "Then I thought maybe Abraham had done it for the money, but we learned he wasn't to inherit, and unless he's been hiding some serious acting abilities all these years, I believe he's genuinely distraught. Whatever else Queenie might have been, she was an excellent wife, and she'd found a true match in Abraham. He was quite indulgent when it came to her exploits, and I feel like a monster for considering him in the first place. Now I'm at a loss."

That was the last Franny had to say on the subject, and when she'd gone, Vera practically dragged Rosemary out the door. "I'm frightfully late, and Frederick is likely to be cross with me, but I had to hear Franny's side of things."

CHAPTER FOURTEEN

Elsie Fletcher arrived at Woolridge House to find an irritated Frederick leaning against a stone column, smoking a cigarette and speaking with Desmond. The way Frederick watched the door, tilting his head every so often and leaning sideways for a better view, portrayed a man who had been waiting for quite some time.

As she'd just come downstairs with her sketch book, Rosemary was on hand to note Elsie's arrival with her son, Nigel, and Amelia, the woman Vera had laughingly referred to as the *randy nanny*. Why on earth it should take both Elsie and the nanny to supervise two healthy boys was a mystery, but Rosemary shrugged off the uncharitable thought, telling herself that as a childless woman, she ought not to judge.

Amelia locked eyes coquettishly with Desmond, living up to Vera's snide moniker. Heat flared between the pair for a long moment, and when Desmond turned away, he looked as though he'd been struck by lightning.

Finally, Vera materialized, greeted Frederick with a

kiss on the cheek, and dragged him away. Left to his own devices, Desmond wandered off in the opposite direction, his expression thoughtful.

Elsie, Nigel, and Amelia followed Rosemary into the dining room, where Nelly had just finished up with luncheon with his mother.

"Miss Amelia!" Nelly shouted, launching himself, as he tended to do, full force into the nanny's arms. "Nan says we have to play outside today because I made a biiiig mess, and now she has to clean up the nursery. Won't you take us down to the pond? I learned how to skip rocks the other day!"

Proving herself willing, Amelia took both boys by the hand and only nodded when she heard Elsie call an order after her. "Nigel is not to have any sweets." Judging by his husky appearance, it was a constant battle.

"Hello, Stella. It's nice to see you," Elsie said, her own cheeks turning a pale shade of pink. "And Rosemary as well, of course. I didn't expect you to stay on so long after the fête. Are you headed back to London soon?"

"As soon as all this murder business is put behind us, I'll return," Rosemary explained.

Again, Elsie flushed. "Of course, you're investigating the murder, and you wouldn't like to leave your family at a time like this." She glanced towards one of the dining room chairs as if deciding whether she should sit or not and then said, "I'll just leave Amelia with Nigel then and let you ladies get back to your day."

"Don't be silly," Stella said, having caught her sister's eye. "Please, stay and have some tea. Isn't Vera floating around here somewhere as well?"

"She and Frederick are out and about doing god only knows what," Rosemary explained, "and Mother is in the village shopping, so it's just the three of us. Do stay, Elsie." She would have preferred not to be forced into an afternoon of awkward conversation; however, getting a line on the enigmatic Elsie was of a higher priority. It seemed she had been given the opportunity to interrogate two suspects in one day, and she wasn't prepared to look a gift horse in the mouth.

Since Elsie stopped twittering and seemed pleased at the invitation, Rosemary decided she'd made the right choice.

"All right then." Elsie took a seat at the table. "I suppose you didn't expect all this treachery when you agreed to attend a modest village fête." It wasn't quite a question, but Rosemary answered anyway.

"No, I certainly didn't, though I probably ought to have." At Elsie's quizzical expression, she explained, "Murder seems to follow me everywhere these days."

"But isn't it exciting, in a rather macabre sort of way? Not like being a wife and mother, though, of course, I do so love my family. Still—murder, intrigue, fabulous London parties, and international travel make your life sound far more scintillating than mine."

Rosemary allowed a wry smile to cross her face. "You do realize you're smack in the middle of a murder investigation yourself, don't you? Intrigue in a small village is far more scandalous than it is in the city, since everyone knows one another. Not so in London, where we hardly recognize more than a handful of our neighbors. People move in and out in a constant flow, never giving one a chance to feel as though one is part of a community."

Elsie frowned. "That sounds far lovelier than only socializing with the same group of women one's whole life."

If she wasn't mistaken, Rosemary noted an element of wistfulness in Elsie's tone. That, taken with the way the woman's fingers worried at the trim of her dress near the collar, was a sign of her true feelings.

"Ah, yes, I suppose that's true. The pickings in Pardington are rather slim, aren't they?" Rosemary deftly maneuvered the conversation back around to Queenie and her tight-knit group, though admittedly, human nature being what it was, she needn't have tried overly hard. "I have noticed that you stand apart from the group at times," Rosemary said, trying to remain tactful. "Brave of you."

The woman took the comment with grace and smiled. "I'm assuming you mean that as a compliment."

"She certainly does," Stella trilled, widening Elsie's smile. With that, the ice thawed even more, making conversation easier than Rosemary had expected.

Elsie relaxed into her seat and explained, choosing her words carefully. "Queenie did tend to make things … difficult. I do hate to speak ill of the dead, but I refuse to eulogize her, and Queenie was mean to the bone. The other women aren't so bad when you get them one on one, and we do all have children around the same age. Common bonds, you understand."

"Well, I, for one, certainly do. Most of the Oxford University wives are older than me by quite a few years, Leonard being such a prodigy and all." Stella spoke of her husband proudly, and Rosemary felt a pang of jealousy mixed with elation that her sister was so happy. "They treat me well enough, I suppose, but we don't have much to talk about."

The conversation continued, and as Elsie warmed up, Rosemary realized she quite liked the woman. Without Olive and Minnie's influence, she proved to be intelligent, down-to-earth, and of good humor.

"I simply can't believe this murder business. Whether Queenie was a pill or not, she didn't deserve to be murdered," Elsie said sometime later, having circled back around to scandal. "However, it seems as though her … demeanor might have made a number of enemies—and created a number of suspects as well."

Rosemary hesitated, trying to decide how much information she should reveal, and finally decided to err on the side of caution. Stella, somewhat more comfortable with Elsie, went off on a tangent.

"Rosemary says everyone is a suspect until proved otherwise. It doesn't look good, does it that Franny is the one who benefited from Queenie's death?"

"No," Elsie said slowly, "though I find it highly unlikely she'd stoop so low as to murder her own cousin. She always allowed Queenie much more leniency than she ought to have done. Of the lot of us, she was the only one rarely bothered by Queenie's behavior. I did notice she'd little patience for the jabs about her intentions with Mr. Murray Alden. In fact, Queenie goaded Franny about the man the morning of the fête."

Stella and Rosemary exchanged a glance. Here was a chance to learn something new.

"Was there any truth to the implication? My mother

seems to think Mr. Alden a man of good character, so what would be the harm if he and Franny were to engage in romantic pursuits?"

Taking a moment to think, Elsie paused with her teacup halfway to her mouth. "Why, none at all, I suppose." The teacup made the return trip to its saucer, touching down with a clinking sound. "Providing Queenie was the one to make the suggestion, and Franny has never been very good at dissembling."

Dissembling struck Rosemary as such an odd word to choose that she was forced to ask for an explanation. "Whatever do you mean by that?"

Leaning forward as if to keep anyone from hearing, Elsie owned up. "If we wanted a thing badly enough, the easiest way to keep the peace was to let Queenie think whatever we wanted was her very own idea. Took some doing sometimes, I don't mind telling you, but saved an awful lot of time and even a few tantrums."

"Did Franny object to deceiving Queenie on principle?" While Vera might have considered resorting to similar machinations when Rosemary had been in the depths of her grief over Andrew, she'd never gone quite so far as to carry them out. It wouldn't be sporting, nor the mark of a true friendship.

"No." Elsie turned thoughtful. "Not as such. She just wasn't very good at being persuasive and not nearly clever enough to put anything past Queenie."

Trying to get it all straight in her mind, Rosemary said, "There was nothing of a personal nature between Franny and Mr. Alden, is that correct?"

"I suppose not, but we did see her talking to him at the fête, so perhaps."

Rosemary was on the verge of asking Elsie what sorts of things she'd had to find a way around Queenie to accomplish, but before she had a chance, Amelia and the two boys returned.

"Nigel isn't feeling well," Nelly informed the room loudly. "He's having pains in his middle."

"Then I think it's best if we take him home and put him to bed." Elsie rested a hand on her son's forehead to check for fever. "Amelia, would you see to getting him settled in the car, please."

"Yes, of course."

When Amelia and young Nigel had gone, Elsie turned to Rosemary and Stella and said, "I expect she'll find herself a husband and leave my service before the year is out. A woman who looks like that won't stay a nanny forever. Nor one who doesn't always know her place. I expect Nigel shall miss her frightfully."

Elsie's tone clearly implied she would not miss Amelia. Rallying, Elsie said her goodbyes, and once she was out the door, Stella turned to Nelly.

"I am quite certain I detect the scent of butterscotch on your breath. How many boiled sweets did Nigel eat?"

Without thinking, Nelly answered, "Only one or two. Not more than four."

Rosemary stifled a snicker. "Dear one, it's time to come and pose for Auntie Rose," she declared instead. He grimaced but followed along behind her anyway, giving Stella a much-needed break. She thanked her sister and tottered off.

"Will I have to sit still for a long, long time?" Nelly asked when she'd gone, his tone dropping into a whine.

Rosemary shook her head. "Not too terribly long, my

dear, though I suspect still longer than you'd like. However, when we're done, we'll have a lovely painting of you to hang in Granddad's study with the rest of the Woolridge family. Won't that be swell?"

Nelly capitulated. "I suppose so. Do I get a treat if I sit very still?" he asked, full, as ever, with questions.

"You're quite an inquisitive one, aren't you?" Rosemary said wryly. At Nelly's baffled expression, she explained, "That means you like to know a lot of things."

"You mean like nosy?" he asked, his eyes narrowed.

Rosemary laughed. "Well, that's one way of putting it." She set him on the chair that she had picked out, with great deliberation, for the purpose of the portrait.

"What is this on your face?" Rosemary asked, wiping off a smudge of brown that could have been dirt but she suspected was chocolate. "Did you have more treats hidden somewhere? I know you heard Miss Elsie saying that Nigel wasn't allowed to have sweets."

Nelly lowered his eyes guiltily and refused to meet his aunt's gaze.

"Nelly," she prodded, using as stern a voice as she could muster. "Tell me the truth."

His cherubic face stared back at her, almost breaking her resolve, but she steeled herself against it. How Stella managed him day in and day out, Rosemary couldn't say, but she suspected that Nelly would become even more of a handful as the years passed, and he realized just how taken in by him they all were.

"Father gave Mother a chocolate box," he explained finally. "Mother isn't fond of chocolate."

Rosemary suspected there was more to the story, and

rightly so. "Where have you been stashing them?" she asked, again in that stern tone. "You'll need to show me."

Nelly's lips twisted to one side, and he appeared to be making a decision. "All right," he said. "I'll show you."

His little legs flashed as he hopped off the chair and marched out of the library and down the corridor to the parlor. Rosemary followed him to one corner, where a bank of cabinets was set into the wall. Inside the empty cupboard, which was tall and wide enough for a boy Nelly's size to curl up cross-legged, she noticed a discrepancy in the wood. Sure enough, Nelly reached down and pulled up the false bottom, revealing a hidden cache of what a young boy would consider valuable treasure.

Empty sweet wrappers made up the majority of the find, but upon further inspection, Rosemary noted several smooth rocks, a few bits of twine, and with horror, the skull of a small animal, most likely a mouse.

"You've been quite busy, haven't you?" she asked, and quirked an eyebrow. Stella's words on her first day at Woolridge House came flooding back. She'd mentioned that with Frederick's help, Nelly had discovered all the nooks and crannies the manor had to offer. "Where is the rest of it?"

Nelly knew he'd been cornered, that there was nothing left to do but make a full confession. Instead of becoming disgruntled by the order, he took great pride in showing her all of his secret areas. After the parlor, he led her upstairs to a hidey hole behind the maid's broom cupboard, another in her father's study, a third beneath the trim surrounding the butler's pantry, and finally to a

131

loose block in the lower wall of the solarium. There, she discovered just how duplicitous her nephew could be.

"You've pilfered yourself quite a collection." Anything, Rosemary judged, that might catch the eye of a young boy had ended up in one of Nelly's hidden caches. Sticks, stones, a shed snakeskin, an empty headache powder container. Picking up a stick in case there were more skulls hidden away, she poked and prodded her way through Nelly's treasures.

There, amongst the spoils, lay Queenie Baker's gold-plated cigarette holder. Rosemary picked it up and examined it, then pierced Nelly with a stare. "When and where did you find this, little love?"

"Um ... I'm not certain," the boy replied, averting his gaze much the same way he had earlier, when the chocolate on his face had been discovered.

"I think you are," Rosemary said bluntly. "Was it the day of the fête?"

He nodded, tears welling up in his blue eyes. "Did I do something really bad?"

"No, dear. You didn't. You were just being a child. However, it's important that you found this, and you're going to have to explain yourself very clearly and carefully."

The last thing Rosemary wanted to do was call Max. She'd tried very hard not to think about him all day, to push the conversation from the evening before out of her thoughts, but there was no denying what must be done. With a sigh, she made the necessary call, instructing Max to come to Woolridge House later that evening when the rest of the family would be present.

In the interim, she abandoned the plan of painting

Nelly's portrait, instead accompanying the child around the outside of the manor, where he proudly displayed his ability to climb trees, secrete himself in the tunnels formed at the base of hedges, and crawl into any nook he'd found on the property.

"You've got to be more careful near the pond, little one," she chided when he nearly toppled into the water from his perch on the rock near its edge. Rosemary vowed to talk with her sister about Nan, and the fact that, considering everything she'd learned that day, it seemed Nelly went unsupervised for much of the time. The prospect of having to relieve Nan of her duties wouldn't please Stella in the slightest, and Rosemary decided she'd hoist this particular task onto her mother's shoulders.

CHAPTER FIFTEEN

Max arrived earlier than expected, coming in just behind Frederick and Vera to find the entire family crowded around Nelly in the parlor. Laid out on the coffee table were the purloined pieces from his trove of treasures. The cigarette holder Rosemary had put aside, thinking that if it turned out to be the murder weapon there could still be traces of poison coating the tip. Young Nelly sat on the edge of his seat, excitement etched across his face despite the stern talking-to he'd received from Stella upon seeing the evidence of his perfidy.

"It seems we have two amateur sleuths in the house," Frederick said, clapping Nelly on his shoulder with pride. "The little man may have found something that furthers the investigation, mightn't you Nelly?"

"Frederick Woolridge, you stop it right now," Evelyn intoned. "Your encouragement is precisely why your nephew thinks scavenging the house is a grand idea. Any evidence that was on that cigarette holder is likely gone by now thanks to Nelly, and more importantly, if it was the murder weapon, he could have been poisoned as well."

That slapped the smile right off Frederick's face.

"Nelly, dear, did you put your mouth on it?" She'd already asked him the same question at least seven times, but apparently Evelyn felt one more was in order. Perhaps she believed he'd give a different answer with Max present, but Nelly vehemently denied having touched the holder to his lips.

"Boys will be boys, Evelyn," Max said gently. "However, I understand your frustration. Why don't we see if we can get to the heart of the matter, shall we?" He deftly maneuvered Evelyn into silence, and then turned to the boy. "Nelly, I'll need you to tell me everything that you saw the day of the fête, including where you found Mrs. Baker's cigarette holder. Can you do that for me?"

Nelly swallowed hard and nodded, his eyes the size of saucers. "Yes, sir," he said seriously.

"Now, tell me what you did the day of the party, and don't leave anything out." Max took out a pencil and a pad of paper, then waited patiently while Nelly took a deep breath, scrunched up his nose in thought, and finally launched into his tale.

"Well, Nanny woke me up and took me down to the dining room, where Granddad was eating breakfast. I had some bacon, toast, and half a boiled egg. It was runny, and I didn't like it. I wanted flapjacks with honey, but Cook said no, she was too busy. Mama was busy helping Gran, and so Nan took me down to the pond. When we came back, she said it was time for a nap. I couldn't fall asleep, so I waited until she began to snore, and then I went to have an adventure." Nelly finally took a breath.

His eyes flicked towards his mother, who nodded calmly and indicated that he should continue. Reprimanding him at this juncture wouldn't have been effective, but from the look on Stella's face, it was clear she intended to have an entirely different conversation with her son when all this was over.

"I sneaked into the solar … solari … the sunroom at the back of the house to see if I'd left any sweets there, but Auntie Rose caught me and sent me back to the nursery. That's when Mrs. Baker …" he stopped, his bottom lip beginning to tremble, "Mrs. Baker gave me some butterscotches, and I went back to bed. Is that why she died? Because she did something naughty too? Auntie Rose said I wasn't supposed to be eating candies …"

Stella moved to where Nelly sat and put her arm around him. "Oh, dear, no. What happened to Mrs. Baker had nothing to do with that, or with you. We're trying to find out what happened to her, and you might know something that could help us. Just keep telling Inspector Max what you saw."

He sniffed, seemed reassured, and continued. "Well, when I woke up from my nap, Nan was still asleep. I went out onto the roof and climbed down Gran's rose ladder. I think I broke some of the flowers, and I knew she'd be mad at me, so I went around to the potting shed to see if there was any flower glue in there. I wanted to put them back together. But I couldn't find anything to help, so I came back through the garden. When I went by the bench out there, I saw something shiny on the ground and picked it up."

"Was this what you picked up?" Max asked, showing the cigarette holder to Nelly.

"Yes, that was it. I think it was Mrs. Baker's. I saw her using it once before. I was going to give it back to her, but then …"

"I understand," Max said. "Now, do you remember seeing anyone or anything else while you were near that bench? Did you see Mrs. Baker, any of her friends, or any of the staff?"

Nelly thought about it, his eyes going a little misty, and finally said, "No. She wasn't there then. I only saw that protection man, the one who beats around the hedgerows, but he was way out by the stables doing something to the grass. I heard them,"—he pointed to his grandmother, aunt, and Vera—"talking about a baroness, and Gran was using her stern voice."

"That's very good, Nelly. You've been a big help to the case." Max held out his hand and Nelly shook it, his expression indicating that he took the whole process very seriously.

"Can I go up to my room now?" he asked.

Stella said, "Yes, of course, dear," and heaved herself off her chair. Evelyn rose a moment later, muttering something about having to use her stern voice with Nan.

"I'd hate to be in her shoes right now," Frederick commented cheerfully as his mother opened the door to leave. "Mother is going to have poor Nan's head on a platter after this."

Desmond grunted. "Your mother may need to be reminded of how many times we were able to slip out as children. I rather admire his tenacity. He's a wily little one, that boy, and your Nan is not as young as she once was."

"You needn't remind me of anything of the sort." Evelyn poked her head back into the library and chided Desmond in the motherly tone she used on all her children—him included. "Just because you and Frederick were naughty little devil children doesn't mean Nelly will end up that way. You two need to stop encouraging his behavior."

With a cheerful nod, Desmond acquiesced, but he sent a wink in Frederick's direction. Evelyn saw it and grimaced at him, which also did nothing whatsoever to dim his mood.

A few more moments passed in speculation of whether Nan might be let go, and in gratefulness that Nelly had not been harmed by his adventures.

"Stella's domestic woes are not our concern right now," Rosemary said. "We just learned a valuable piece of information. We know the cigarette holder wasn't the murder weapon. It couldn't have been," she explained, "because if it were, she would have been dead when Nelly found it. Isn't that right, Max? According to the type of poison that was used."

"Yes," Max said slowly, "your theory holds water. The pathologist said that death would have been quick due to the amount of digitalis already in Mrs. Baker's system. I'd still prefer to have the cigarette holder tested, but it's safe to assume it wasn't the tool with which the poison was delivered. Which means we're back to that blasted missing flask. I'll take this with me, and if anything else comes up, you give me a call."

So saying, Max departed without stopping to talk with Rosemary in private as per his usual custom. She wondered if their conversation the evening before had affected him as much as it had her, and vowed again to dwell on the idea later, with Vera and a bucket full of gin. She heard her mother descend to the ground floor and bid Max goodbye before returning to the library.

"I suppose there's nothing more to be done," she said, "so I'll just have Stella and Nelly's dinner sent upstairs. The rest of you can meet me in the dining room." She kissed her husband on the forehead perfunctorily and tottered back into the entrance hall, her brow still furrowed and her eyes still dark and stormy.

The rest of the group filed out behind her, and Rosemary let out a sigh of relief when she counted the place settings and confirmed that Vera hadn't been forgotten this evening. Mouthwatering scents wafted in from the kitchen as the cook lumbered through the door and deposited a platter of lamb tikka masala onto the table. Rosemary closed her eyes, and, with pleasure, inhaled the combination of ginger, garlic, and something else she couldn't quite identify.

"This smells quite appetizing, Mother," she said appreciatively. "There's something new, but I can't quite detect the seasoning."

Evelyn preened. "It's a new recipe. Mr. Murray Alden gave a talk on the history of plants used as seasonings at one of our society meetings. He suggested some combinations for use in favored recipes to spice them differently."

They all tucked in, dragging forkfuls of tender lamb through the creamy, fragrant sauce while the debate regarding Queenie's murder raged around the table.

"My money is on the husband," Frederick declared.

"A simple case of mistaken belief. He assumed his wife had left him all her money, and since she was such an insufferable woman, decided to get rid of her and run off with the cash. Perhaps he even has a little filly on the side."

"Bollocks!" Desmond retorted then apologized to Evelyn when she flinched at his choice of words. "You met the man, didn't you? Not an ounce of creativity in that one, mark my words. I suspect if he'd wanted to get rid of her, he'd have arranged some sort of accident. Pushed her off a ledge, perhaps, though I doubt very highly he'd have the stomach for murder."

"Then who?" Frederick fired back indignantly.

Desmond didn't hesitate with his answer. "Franny, of course. The simplest explanation is usually the correct one, isn't it? She might have found out the truth of Queenie's will and then decided she couldn't take another day with that harpy. Here's her opportunity to get away from those wretched women. I find it far more likely she's the one with a clandestine lover. She certainly showed no interest in Freddie here, and women typically do."

That got Vera's attention. She raised an eyebrow at Desmond, shifted her gaze to Frederick, and then, instead of shooting a biting remark in his direction, erupted into a fit of coughing.

"Relax, my darling. I only have eyes for you," Frederick assured her when she finally stopped gasping. "Old Des overstated himself. I bumped into the girl whilst getting a nice drink to take the taste of tea out of my mouth. The look she gave me was enough to wither stone. She pushed past me on her way back to the table without a backward glance. Desmond's assumption that all women fall at my feet is simply erroneous. I've been turned down as many times as not."

Rosemary didn't think his math was quite accurate; she'd seen the way women took to her brother, and it was somewhat surprising that one who, by all accounts, was on the hunt for a husband wouldn't have seized the opportunity to flirt with an attractive, unmarried man. But then, Frederick hadn't been the only one of those in attendance.

"Nelly saw Mr. Alden roaming hedges that day, and Elsie says Franny was talking to him before teatime."

"Perhaps ... perh—" Vera struggled to get the words out as she was overcome with some sort of fit that had her shifting in her seat. A few red blotches had appeared on her cheek and more on her neck, the spots rapidly combining into large, swollen welts. Her eyes widened in panic, and she pointed to the dish in front of her. "What ... in ... this?"

Evelyn rose from her seat, bustled into the kitchen, and returned with a piece of paper. "It's cream, garlic, ginger, nutmeg, cinnamon—"

"Cinnamon?" Rosemary squeaked. "Vera can't have cinnamon! We must call the doctor! Mother, how could you have made such a mistake?"

"I—I—" Evelyn stammered, her feet apparently rooted to the floor.

Cecil rose, pushed his chair back forcefully, and strode towards the entrance hall. "I'll get Dr. Leidner on the phone. Evelyn, help the children get Vera upstairs." His voice held notes of disappointment and irritation; it seemed as though the tables had turned, and now his wife was the one on thin ice.

"Did you do this on purpose?" Rosemary's hands landed on her hips, hard, as she demanded an answer from her mother.

Evelyn blanched, then turned nearly the color of Vera's lips as she balked. "Of course not. Why on earth would I do such a horrid thing?"

"You have treated her abominably since we arrived. I've kept quiet out of respect for Vera's wishes, but it's not like you to forget about your guests' aversions," Rosemary replied bluntly. "So, did you?"

Her mother's eyes widened, but before she could answer Frederick boomed, "It's not important right now. What's important is ensuring Vera gets treatment immediately."

Everyone in Pardington knew the story of Brian Edward-Jones, who had developed hives after being stung by a honeybee and died not half an hour later.

"Stop your bickering and do something to help!" He interrupted the argument, but the glare he sent in Evelyn's direction assured them all that the conversation was far from over.

CHAPTER SIXTEEN

"Are you certain she's going to be all right?" Rosemary asked the doctor while Frederick sat at Vera's bedside, holding her limp hand in his.

Dr. Leidner nodded. "She'll be perfectly fine, though it's a good thing you called as soon as you noticed the reaction. It could have been far more serious. I've given her something for the itching." He handed Rosemary a bottle of pink lotion. "To be applied liberally, and I've given her a powder to help her sleep through the worst of it. I'll come around tomorrow to check on her. Call if her condition worsens," he said and left the three of them alone.

"I can't believe Mother," Rosemary ranted as she paced. "I know she doesn't care for Vera—never has—but this goes beyond the pale."

"Leave it alone, Rose," Frederick said, though his voice still had an edge of irritation to it. "She's acting out of love, however misguided."

"You sound like Max," Rosemary said, huffing out a breath and finally taking a seat on the bed next to her dearest friend. "What is it about men and their mothers, anyway?"

Frederick's mouth contorted into a grimace. "That's an age-old question I don't have an answer for, Rosie. However, I suspect she'll come around. She'll have to, won't she?" He softened as he gazed at Vera.

"It's serious, then?" Rosemary asked, although she suspected she already knew the answer to *that* question.

Her brother quirked an eyebrow. "I'm completely besotted, but you did know that, didn't you? I can't explain it. Three months ago, I thought of Vera as an irritating, albeit beautiful, thorn in my side. Now I've come to realize I was every kind of a fool. I'm going to marry her, if she'll have me."

"Perhaps you could wait until the swelling has gone down and this murder has been solved to pop the question," Rosemary replied wryly.

"So you support my decision? You think we'd make a good match?" Frederick asked quietly.

Rosemary stared at him in disbelief. "Did you ever doubt that was the case?" she asked.

"No, not really," Frederick said, brightening. "I merely wondered if it was too soon for you."

"This has been years in the making; the two of you were just too stubborn to admit it. Whether I'm lonely or not, I can still be happy for the both of you. Furthermore, I'm thrilled at the thought of Vera as my sister-in-law. I couldn't think of anything that would make me happier. However, you all need to stop handling me with kid gloves, and Fred, for goodness' sake, please stop attempting to betroth me to your chums."

He snickered and nodded. "I want you to be happy,

Rosie."

"Yes, I realize that, Freddie dear, and I appreciate the sentiment if not your methods. I've finally shaken Teddy Barton off, but poor Des is still attached to my skirt hems. It's quite a lot of pressure, and I'm afraid if I don't get some peace, I might lose my grip on my sanity."

Frederick appraised his sister and, noting the rueful expression on her face, determined she was only joking. He raised an eyebrow and poked back. "Are you certain you haven't already? I did hear that you threatened Queenie with bodily harm shortly before she was murdered."

"Shut up, Fred," she replied, the tension that had built in her chest finally ebbing. "The woman might have been a terror and a tyrant, but she wasn't worth the effort of murder. At least not for me. I have to wonder, though, whether a mental breakdown didn't have something to do with it. She had an uncanny ability to press on a person's weak points until she broke them, and that little group of hers wasn't as close as they appear to have been."

"Why do you dislike those women so deeply?" Frederick wanted to know.

Rosemary considered carefully before answering. "I could have been one of them. That's what bothers me so much. I find them vapid, irritating, and completely out of touch with the times. I'm no revolutionary, of course, and I did get married right out of art school. I don't have a real reason to feel superior to them, and yet I do. It makes me feel as though I'm being prideful, and I've always considered too much pride a character flaw."

"You're the least prideful person I know, Rose, and you're not a monster for disliking those women. They're vipers, the lot of them."

"I'm not certain about that," Rosemary said slowly. "Elsie seems all right. She's stuck in with that crowd out of necessity, and Franny isn't so bad either, now that Queenie's gone. It's unsettling to believe they're probably all better off without her. That seems a terrible thing to think, let alone say out loud."

"That's because you're a good person, Rosie, but it doesn't mean it isn't true."

"Everyone has something to give—some good in them—even Queenie. I have to believe that."

Frederick smiled at his sister. "Like I said, you're a good person. Even if Queenie possessed one redeeming quality, it's her fault she left this world with a black mark on her. Perhaps she's found some peace now."

"Perhaps," Rosemary sighed. She felt suddenly very tired, and her eyes drooped.

"We'll figure this out, Rosie, and there are good things on the horizon for all of us," Frederick promised. "Why don't you lie down and rest?"

She agreed, and crawled into bed beside Vera, watching her friend's slow inhales and exhales until she fell into a dreamless sleep.

***

During breakfast the next morning, there was a ruckus.

"Where is my daughter?" Lorraine Blackburn burst into the dining room at Woolridge House. With her hair

146

in disarray and without a stitch of makeup on her face, she looked older, yet somehow softer than usual. "Why didn't you call me last night, Evelyn?" she demanded harshly.

Evelyn paled and explained that Frederick had taken Vera her breakfast in bed without making another nasty comment upon the impropriety of such familiar actions between an unmarried couple. Without another word, Lorraine swooshed back out through the door, nearly wrenching it from its hinges.

"I've never seen Mrs. Blackburn look like that before," Stella commented, staring after her. Nelly continued eating his oatmeal without seeming to notice or care what was going on around him. He'd been on his best behavior after having had his illicit activities brought to light in front of the whole family.

Rosemary rose from her chair and followed Lorraine's path towards the entrance hall. "You most likely never will again, Stella." Upstairs, she realized Frederick hadn't quite managed the deed after all.

"Get out." Vera's declared loudly. "Frederick Woolridge, don't you dare poke your head in this room again."

Using the word dare in front of Frederick never went to plan, so of course, he stuck his head back inside. "Here now, what's all the fuss? I've come to bring you sustenance, such as one might need after a night of feeling poorly. Is that a reason to throw things at me?"

Since a small pillow bounced off the edge of the door, Frederick got his answer.

"Go away," Vera ordered again, and this time Frederick complied, but not before handing the breakfast tray to Rosemary. "She's gone daft, did you notice?"

Putting a hand to her mouth to stop a giggle at her brother's bafflement, Rosemary filled him in on the gaffe. "You great lout. She's feeling unattractive, being as she's been covered in blotches and pink lotion, and when I came downstairs, her hair looked like a home for nesting rats. Come back in a few minutes, and you'll get a different reception, I suspect."

When she set the breakfast tray down on the dresser and turned to look at Vera, Rosemary's prediction proved accurate. Lorraine was perched on the edge of the bed, fawning all over her daughter like a mother hen. "Why don't you come home and let me take care of you?" One hand absently smoothed across the raven wing of Vera's hair after each brush stroke settled the silken tresses back into place.

"Rose needs me, Mother. You know that." With a skill only she possessed, Vera fixed her face, applying powder and a touch of rouge without benefit of a mirror. When she was finished, she handed the powder over. "Fix your face, Mother, you look an absolute fright."

"Hmm, yes, I suppose I do," Lorraine replied. "Nonetheless, if Rose needs you, she's welcome to come and stay as long as she likes. I simply don't think it's fair that Evelyn gets to see more of you than I do. And now you're unwell, and I want to ensure you're being looked after."

For once, not being subjected to the prickly way with which Vera usually responded to her, Lorraine let down a little of her guard to admit, "You've scared a year off my life, you know."

To have left the house in such a state said more to

Vera than words, and her expression softened. "I'm sorry. It was never my intent." Smiling, she handed Lorraine the hairbrush as another knock sounded on the door.

"Let me in, Vera. I need to see you," Frederick called through the door.

"Scared him, too." Rosemary finally spoke. "He's in a right state."

"Come ahead, then, you silly man."

Frederick came through the door as if he were a mouse trying to tiptoe past the family cat, so unsure was he of his reception.

Vera glanced at Frederick, and Rosemary watched as a slow smile lit her face. "Freddie is taking quite good care of me, Mother."

"And there lies the rest of your conviction, I'd say," Lorraine sighed. "You two can't stand to be away from one another; I can see that plain as day."

Frederick flushed, and Vera smiled.

"I suppose that settles it," Lorraine said matter-of-factly. "Now why don't you tell me what's happened?"

Rosemary shooed Frederick back downstairs, where she assumed he would pass the word of Vera's recovery on to the rest of the family. Vera's mother made room for her to sit on the edge of the bed. "You'd better let me explain; Vera isn't going to be entirely honest with you, I suspect."

Vera tossed Rosemary a quelling look, which she ignored.

"It's my mother. They're not quite getting along. Mind you, I don't think she asked the cook to put cinnamon in the tikka masala on purpose—that would be a step too far even for her—but it's fair to say she isn't as thrilled with the match between Vera and Freddie as the rest of us are."

"I can handle Evelyn's displeasure," Vera sputtered. "There was no need to drag my mother into the middle of this spat. What can she possibly do or say that won't make the situation worse? If she defends me, your mother will blame me for breaking up a friendship. If she defends Evelyn, I'll—well, I don't know what I'll do, but crying or yelling will be involved."

Lorraine wisely came down on neither side, as there was nothing to be gained by making a choice.

"Her displeasure is one thing; the way she's been acting is another." Rosemary explained how the two of them had gone back and forth, how Vera had given as good as she'd got.

"I suggest," Lorraine said, looking at Rosemary with a hint of a twinkle in her eye, "you'd be far better off to join me here on the neutral side of the war zone. This is something they'll have to work through without our help or protection."

"You think we ought to let them keep clawing at one another? You don't think we should do something about it?"

"I appreciate your concern, dear, but I raised Vera to stand up for herself—to fight her own battles. I believe it's given her a strength of character which many envy. Let me ask you this—if your beau's mother didn't like you, would you want her to be forced to like you, or to come to that conclusion on her own?"

Lorraine's comment was like a punch to the gut, and

more so because she had no idea Rosemary might be in a similar position. Would she want Max to force his mother to approve of their relationship should they ever decide to start one? The answer was a decided no. Perhaps that was what Max had meant when he'd stated his opinion regarding harmony within a family. Harmony sounded quite nice to Rosemary, and now that she thought about it, dealing with a feud between Evelyn and Vera wasn't how she wanted to spend her time.

With Mrs. Blackburn's suggestion weighing on her mind, Rosemary left mother and daughter to a moment of peace.

CHAPTER SEVENTEEN

Rosemary had decided that since Vera was being looked after—or, more accurately, watched like a hawk—by Frederick, and Nelly was on his best behavior, it was time to finish the portrait Stella had asked her to paint. She'd fastened on a smock to keep her dress from ruin and was poised to touch brush to canvas when the doorbell rang.

She could have been knocked over by a feather when Bertram ushered Minnie into the solarium and announced, "Mrs. Kitteridge for you, Miss Rose."

"Oh!" Rosemary said, attempting to keep the surprise from her voice and failing miserably. "Nelly dear, why don't you go and find Nan now—and no running about and causing mischief, understand?"

The boy nodded, cast a curious look at Minnie—perhaps wondering if her pockets were also filled with candies—and tripped out through the back corridor.

"What can I do for you, Minnie?" Rosemary asked and noted the pinch-nosed reaction the woman had to her question. She hadn't thought Minnie was capable of an internal struggle, but it appeared she was experiencing one. The unlikely pair stood near the front of the solarium, where the rainbow of blooming flowers painted a pretty picture that went unnoticed while Minnie struggled to get her words out.

"I'm sorry to bother you," she said, though the apology didn't quite come across as sincere. "I'd intended to talk with Evelyn, but I suppose you'll do." Her words caused a sharp retort to bubble into Rosemary's throat. She swallowed it and allowed Minnie to continue. "I'd like to put a token next to where Queenie died." She patted her handbag.

While Rosemary would have liked to shoo her off the property, she nodded in understanding. "I'm certain my mother would allow you that, so it's all right with me." She hesitated and then threw caution to the wind. "It seems as though you have something weighing on your mind …"

Minnie appeared thrown by the lack of animosity in Rosemary's voice, and her eyes narrowed with suspicion. "I don't know why you would think I'd reveal my innermost thoughts to you," she replied testily.

Rosemary sighed, counted to five in her head, and said, "I didn't ask you to go shopping with me or gossip over afternoon cocktails, you know."

With a roll of her eyes, Minnie acquiesced. "We've just been to see Franny—Olive, Elsie, and me—and she's an absolute wreck. Until Queenie's murder is solved, I fear she won't be able to rest. I realize we've never been friends and that you don't think very highly of me, or any of the rest of us, but I do have a heart, and I can't stand to see Franny like this."

Rosemary led Minnie out onto the terrace and down the path to where it forked. She had enough respect to allow Minnie a modicum of privacy, and so she stopped there and boldly asked, "Does your concern mean you don't believe Franny is responsible for Queenie's death?"

"I find it highly unlikely, despite what she had to gain. Queenie kept her own counsel. I doubt Franny was aware she'd been willed the money, and even if she was, she wouldn't have killed her for it. Franny doesn't have a vindictive bone in her body. Not like some people I know." At that, Minnie's expression changed to one of malice.

"Do you remember in our first year of secondary school when someone slipped laxative into Queenie's drink? Nobody ever owned up to the deed, but I know it was Elsie Fletcher. She'd found Queenie *socializing* with her then beau, and punished Queenie in retaliation."

"Are you quite positive?" Rosemary asked, her mind whirling at the thought of Elsie being so duplicitous.

Minnie pierced her with a look of irritation. "Yes, I'm quite positive. I wouldn't have said I know for a fact if I wasn't certain. I can see you don't believe it. Perhaps you might if you weren't prejudiced against me. I suppose you think Elsie is a nice, respectable woman, but you're wrong. She's got a mean streak a mile wide; she's just more adept at covering it than Queenie was."

"It seems to me you all have a mean streak," Rosemary said, keeping her tone even and her eyes locked on Minnie's.

The woman raised an eyebrow and glared back at her. "Am I to assume you've always followed every rule?

That you've never said a bad word about anyone? That you don't have your own opinions that aren't always charitable? I saw the way you spoke to Queenie the day we saw you at the dress shop. You and Vera look down your noses at the rest of us. You think we're simple-minded because we chose to marry, have children, and bring them up in the same place we were brought up. What is so wrong with that? Why are you any better because you went to London and got married? I expect you intended to have children before your husband died. You're just like us, whether you want to admit it or not."

Hearing those words come out of Minnie's mouth took Rosemary aback. The woman was right; she'd spent the entire time here in Pardington feeling quite vindicated in her opinions regarding the choices she'd made as opposed to those of the prevention-society set. Minnie was right, though admitting so made Rosemary's stomach churn with irritation.

"Is there anything else that makes you think Elsie killed Queenie?" Rosemary wanted to know. "Even if she did what you say, it was years ago, and it doesn't necessarily make her a murderer."

"Perhaps not, but Elsie presents two faces to the world, so I'd watch out for her. She manages to keep her temper under wraps, for the most part, but mark my words, you don't know her as well as you think you do."

Rosemary pressed a little harder, her thoughts popping out of her mouth before she could stop them. "Why then, wasn't Elsie angry with her beau? It seems he's the one to blame if he was stepping out on her with Queenie."

Minnie stared, once again, as if she thought Rosemary

might be daft. "I'm quite certain she was—she threw him off immediately. However, Queenie was her friend, and Elsie thought she deserved to be treated better. She wasn't wrong on that count, but she should have directed her ire towards Olive, as well, since Olive knew all about the deception. Olive always knows more than she lets on. Now, if you don't mind, I'd like to say goodbye to my friend. In private."

"Of course," Rosemary agreed. "You can see yourself out." With that, she left Minnie to it and walked slowly back inside, wondering what else Olive might have kept under wraps.

She wandered up to her room to check on Vera, to find her friend sitting up in bed and looking quite healthy.

"Have you come to spring me from my prison?" Vera asked hopefully. "I've been banished, it seems. Your brother has insisted that none of the staff are to allow me to leave, even though the doctor said I'm fully recovered."

Rosemary sat down on the edge of the bed and shook her head. "You won't find me situating myself on Frederick's bad side. You're stuck here, and it's a good thing, too. I've just had the most unlikely visitor."

She relayed the conversation between herself and Minnie, describing every nuance of the woman's demeanor at Vera's insistence.

"It's one of them, isn't it?" Vera said once Rosemary's narrative had concluded. "Not that I'm surprised, mind you, for who else could it have been? If only that blasted flask had been amongst Nelly's findings. I feel quite certain that's the murder weapon."

"As do I," Rosemary agreed. "But which one?"

Vera shrugged. "Perhaps they're all in it together. Wouldn't that be an interesting twist?"

CHAPTER EIGHTEEN

Rosemary stayed with Vera, discussing the possibilities of the case until Frederick arrived. She closed the door to allow them some privacy and had begun to descend the staircase when a loud bang and a flurry of voices erupted from somewhere below.

One of the maids exited the door at the end of the corridor—the one near the service staircase—tears streaming down her face as she pressed past Rosemary and sprinted up the stairs. Rosemary sighed again and pushed her way into the dining room to find Evelyn, Cecil, and the cook in a standoff.

"I'm sorry, Mrs. Woolridge, but she's the third one this week to give her notice and find another post. I'm afraid you're going to have to call the service and get another girl sent over. I'd recommend doing it quickly because they love to gossip, and it's probably got around by now they're all leaving." That no maid in her right mind would come to work at Woolridge House after hearing about Evelyn's tyranny was implied.

"Never in my life have I employed such insolent staff," Evelyn said, pointing her nose in the air and stalking out of the dining room. She refused to meet her daughter's gaze, but Rosemary could tell Evelyn was on the verge of tears herself.

Cecil tried to smooth things over, and eventually, the cook went back to her duties with the reassurance that he would find a suitable replacement for the maid. "Perhaps you could try speaking with your mother, Rosemary. I've got some work to do in my study," he said, deftly handing off the responsibility.

She found her mother in the parlor, wielding a feather duster and muttering to herself. "I'll just do it all myself. Think I'm so hard to work for, what utter nonsense! These girls today …"

"Mother." Rosemary roused Evelyn's attention and received a glare of reproach in response. It seemed the woman of the house was going to prove more difficult to reason with than little Nelly. "What is going on with you? Is this about the murder or about the preservation society? Perhaps it has to do with Freddie and Vera," she added when her mother sneered at the mention of the preservation society.

Evelyn reared up for a sharp retort, but it fell dead on her lips. She sank into one of the armchairs and flung her arm across her forehead in a dramatic gesture.

"Bring me a brandy, please," she asked and rearranged herself while Rosemary did so. After she drained the glass, she looked her daughter in the eye and said with defeat, "There's nothing I can do about this match, is there?"

"No. Nor should there be. But why would you want to *do something* about it in the first place?" Rosemary asked quietly, trying to keep from sounding frustrated.

"The same reason I have for everything I do. To protect my children. I've already lost one of you to a pointless war."

Rosemary bit down on her cheek to try and hold back tears. It hurt her heart to be so blunt with her grieving mother.

"Do you want to lose another to your own stubbornness?" she said.

"Of course not," Evelyn retorted. "I simply want your brother to find a woman who wants to settle down and give me grandchildren. Someone who won't pull him to the far corners of the earth."

"You mean someone who will stay in Pardington and join your preservation society?" Rosemary asked wryly. "You do realize you're asking for him to end up with someone just like those women when it's likely one of them murdered another."

Evelyn blanched, and the color rose in her cheeks. "I hadn't thought about it like that," she said with a sigh.

"Furthermore, you don't have any idea what kind of woman Vera is now. You still see her as the wild child she once was, but she's changed of late, and I don't believe her desires are as far off from yours as you think they are. Don't avoid the situation; the two of you need to sit down and talk. With civility, like adults."

If Evelyn registered her daughter's insinuation that she was acting like a child, it didn't show. She bit her lip, and then stood, squared her shoulders, and said, "You're absolutely right." She marched out of the parlor, Rosemary watching as she ascended the stairs and knocked on the door to Rosemary's room.

"Frederick, please go and find something else to do. I

160

need to talk with Vera. Alone."

"I'm not—" Head swiveling from one to the other, Frederick found himself having to consider blatantly disobeying his mother to ensure Vera wouldn't be thrown to the wolves. Finally, at Vera's insistence, he nodded and allowed Evelyn to go inside, closing the door in his face.

"We could listen," he said to Rosemary, who shook her head at him.

"You know they have to work this out on their own. Trust me, Vera will be all right. Mother doesn't apologize often, but when she does, it's sincere. Let them talk it out. It's way past time."

Frederick acquiesced and followed Rosemary downstairs. "What makes you think she's apologizing?" he asked, still unsettled.

"Because I made a point she couldn't refute," was all Rosemary would say on the subject. An hour later, Evelyn emerged from Vera's room with a satisfied smile on her face.

"Frederick!" She called his name before she noticed him sitting only a few feet away. "Vera will be down soon, and I expect you to see to her every need. Do I make myself clear? We can't have that delightful girl falling ill again just when she's feeling more herself." So saying, Evelyn spun on her heel and left the room.

Rosemary and Frederick could do no more than stare at each other for several seconds, and then they both began to laugh.

CHAPTER NINETEEN

"Are you certain you're feeling up to coming down for dinner?" Rosemary asked Vera the following evening. "We can send up a tray, you know."

Vera balked at the offer. "I've had quite enough of being alone with my thoughts and more than enough of these four walls."

Since her color was back to normal, her eyes bright with health, and the pall cast by the debacle had been lifted, Vera seemed more her old self.

"I'm glad to see you smiling, even if it is over my discomfort."

"Wild horses couldn't drag me away from the spectacle of your reunion with Max. Was it your mother's idea to invite him to dinner, or Cecil's?"

"Mother's, if you can believe it. Whether it has anything to do with a desire to see me paired with Max, I couldn't say, but it's doubtful. More likely, she wants inside information about Queenie's murder case," Rosemary postulated.

"I can't say I blame her for that." Vera came to Evelyn's defense, causing Rosemary to raise an eyebrow. "Queenie *was* found dead in her own garden; that's reason enough to want the case solved."

Rosemary shrugged. "Reason enough, but not the only reason. She's also an unmitigated gossip who can't resist the urge to meddle."

"Sounds like someone else I know," Vera said wryly.

Ignoring the sassy comment, Rosemary took one last look in the mirror and, deciding she was presentable, gestured for Vera to precede her down the stairs.

Max had already arrived, and he greeted Rosemary warmly, making her wonder if the tension she'd sensed after their last conversation had been all in her imagination. A surge of what felt like hope sprang to her breast, but she kept her expression neutral.

"It's far less tense here than it was last time, isn't it?" he asked under his breath.

For a moment, she thought perhaps he could read her mind, and then realized he was referring to the situation between Vera and Evelyn. She surveyed the scene before her, watched as her mother doted upon Vera, and noted that her friend lit up like a Christmas tree at the attention.

"Yes, they seem to have mended fences, and none too soon for any of us. It was starting to feel like a war zone in here," she whispered back. "You were right, by the way. It's far nicer when everyone gets along."

Max pierced her with an enigmatic look, but only nodded in response.

Cecil rose from his chair, clapped Max on the back, and said, "Hello, young chap, it's good to see you."

"You as well." Max smiled and took the chair Cecil indicated for him, right next to Rosemary. "Evelyn, thank you for asking me to join you for dinner. Mrs. Shropshire makes a wonderful sandwich, but I've been looking forward to a home-cooked meal."

"You're quite welcome. I suppose you don't get many of those, being a single man." She could have winked at Rosemary, and it would have been filled with less innuendo than her suggestive tone.

Max graciously ignored the implication of her words and chuckled. "Entirely too true, Evelyn. Too true. I confess to taking most of my meals at one of the pubs near my flat. Of course, with my mother living in London, I try to stop by at least once a week to share a meal with her."

"A man who loves his mother; that's a rarity these days." She smiled indulgently at Frederick, who had been too focused on attending to Vera's every need that he had yet to comment on the conversation.

"Of course I adore you, Mother," he said with a twinkle in his eye. "Particularly when you're on your best behavior."

"Oh, pishposh, Freddie," Evelyn replied, but the smile didn't leave her face. It seemed all had been set to rights at Woolridge House. Excepting, of course, the outstanding murder investigation that had yet to be concluded.

"Where is Desmond?" Rosemary asked suddenly, realizing there was one fewer guest at the table than usual.

Frederick's eyes flicked to Max briefly. "I don't know, exactly. He said he had other plans for the evening but asked me to wish you all well. I get the feeling old Des is a bit restless these days. I expect he'll be off soon, on some adventure across the seas. All that money his dear old auntie left him will be put to some morally bankrupt use if I'm not quite mistaken."

Rosemary felt a weight coming off her shoulders. She adored Desmond, and he'd been a great comfort to have around these last months. However, his constant doting, combined with her mixed feelings, had become exhausting. If he planned to travel, perhaps he'd finally come to the realization that they weren't a fated match, and things could go back to normal.

Just as dessert was being served, there came a ring from the doorbell. It seemed meals at Woolridge House were destined to be interrupted, and this time the surprise was most unexpected.

"Miss Cole is here to see you," Bertram said to Rosemary. "I've asked her to wait in the parlor."

She frowned. "Oh! How odd."

When Rosemary entered the parlor, it was to find a disheveled-looking Franny perched on the edge of one of the armchairs. Wisps of hair badly needed combing, and her skin was sallow. Red-rimmed eyes sporting black circles underneath gave the impression she'd experienced a string of restless nights, and she wore no makeup to cover the blotches on her cheeks.

"Franny, you look a sight." The words popped out of Rosemary's mouth before she could censor herself. "I'm sorry, I didn't mean that the way it sounded."

"I fear you're correct," Franny said, her eyes sharp despite the rest of her appearance. "I don't know why I'm here, except I feel as though you're probably the only person, at the moment, who I might be able to trust."

Rosemary nodded. "You can," she said solemnly. "I promise. What is it you need to tell me?"

"You see, it's … well …" Franny stuttered to explain. "It's just that … I think I'm going mad!"

That hadn't been what Rosemary had expected Franny to say, and she hadn't a clue how to respond. "You're not mad," she said lamely, cursing herself silently for having been caught off guard and unable to come up with anything other than an unconvincing platitude.

Franny reached into her handbag and retrieved something wrapped in a handkerchief. She passed it to Rosemary, who started when she realized what was inside. It was the missing flask, and, judging by the expression on Franny's face, she knew exactly what it meant for her to have it in her possession.

"Before you ask, it wasn't in with Queenie's things when I left the fête. It wasn't there until yesterday, which means, as I said, that I've lost my mind or someone put it there after the fact. Someone who was in my house—a so-called friend, perhaps."

The consternation on her face, the pain of it, softened Rosemary's heart. In fact, it made her wonder if she was cut out to be a private investigator at all. She found she believed that Franny was telling the truth and made a quick decision.

"You need to speak with Inspector Whittington. He's here now, which is positively fortuitous," she said when Franny paled.

"I came to you because I thought you'd take my side. I thought you'd understand. Instead, you want to turn me in. Do you hate me that much?"

Rosemary used the voice she often found worked best

with Nelly and explained, "Of course not. I believe you're in distress, and I believe there's something fishy going on here. I swear to you, Max—Inspector Whittington—will listen to your story, and he won't rush to judgment."

Franny considered, and finally nodded. "All right, I'll trust you, as it seems I have no other choice."

Rosemary summoned Max, making certain to keep her eye on the parlor door in case Franny changed her mind and decided to make a run for it. She didn't, and Rosemary took it as a good sign. After explaining what Franny had told her so far, Max examined the flask, wrapped it back up, and set it aside.

"You found this in Mrs. Baker's clutch?" he asked.

"Yes," Franny said, "but I'm positive it wasn't there when I left the fête."

Max raised an eyebrow, but otherwise didn't respond. "Who had access to the clutch after you took it home?"

Franny's brow furrowed. "I've been thinking a lot about that, and unless someone gained entry to the house through stealthy means, it had to have been either Abraham or one of the girls. They called on me yesterday. We talked, and later I decided it was time to take care of Queenie's things. I couldn't say whether the flask was there in the interim."

Something about her tone caught both Max and Rosemary's attention. They exchanged a look, and then Max asked, "Are you absolutely certain there was no one else who had access to the handbag?"

Franny flushed and refused to meet his gaze.

"I believe you've been honest up to a point, but you must tell me everything. Otherwise, there's nothing I can do to help you," Max said somewhat harshly.

"The only other person who could have tampered with the handbag was Mr. Murray Alden," she announced reluctantly.

Shocked, Rosemary chose a question that would provide more than one answer. "Where were you keeping it that Mr. Alden had such ready access? Somewhere private?"

Chin snapping up, Franny showed the first hint of fire since she'd begun her confession. "I don't see what business it is of yours, but no, I wasn't keeping the clutch in my bedroom if that is what you're asking."

"I said no such thing."

"No?" Franny tossed her head. "It sounded as though that was exactly the question you were asking. The clutch was sitting on a chair in my drawing-room, so anyone who came to visit could have easily slipped the flask inside."

Max cleared his throat and asked Franny to list those names once more, as he committed them to memory.

"Queenie's last barb to me hit closer to home than she realized, but not enough to make me want to kill her! She was my family, and if we didn't always get on, that was between us. She had her reasons for acting the way she did, and I didn't often take her words personally."

Rosemary doubted very much that was truly the case; harsh words from a stranger were a lot easier to shrug off than those of a trusted friend or family member. Her conviction that Franny was telling the truth wavered slightly, and she got the impression Max felt the same way.

"I'm in love with Murray," Franny continued, "and

he's in love with me. We're to be married, and I intend to follow him across the country, assisting him with his work. The money Queenie left me is a boon, certainly. It will allow us to do whatever we wish, but I'd have been just as happy without it. Murray doesn't even know about the money yet, and for that reason, I don't believe he has anything to do with Queenie's death. I suspect you'll have to follow up regardless."

"I certainly will," Max admitted. "Is there anything else—anything at all—that might point to who wanted to hurt your cousin?"

"Perhaps," Franny said slowly. "However, I'm reluctant to point the finger in any direction. All my friends have reason to want Queenie silenced. Olive has always wanted to be the so-called leader of the group, and she disliked having to kowtow to Queenie. She was rather agitated when the girls came to visit, but that was nothing unexpected."

With her confession out of the way, Franny settled more deeply in her seat and searched her memory for possible clues as to who had the most to gain from the murder.

"Minnie hardly says a word, but I know she was getting tired of Queenie's shenanigans. Something between the two of them changed recently; they weren't as close as they used to be, and I believe I know what it might have been. I believe this business with Elsie's nanny was the last straw for Minnie."

A spark kindled in Rosemary's intuition. "What business with Elsie's nanny?"

"You really do intend to force me to speak ill of my deceased cousin, don't you?" Franny snapped.

As Rosemary had yet to hear anyone speak of Queenie in any other way, she dismissed the protest as spurious.

"Let me ask you this—would you want a nanny who looked like Amelia living in your home, within easy reach of your husband?"

Given Amelia's ability to draw a man's attention, Rosemary was ashamed to say her answer would have been no. Andrew hadn't been the type to stray, but Amelia would be a temptation not worth testing.

Franny must have seen the hesitation because she smirked. "Well, it seems the girl couldn't keep a post—too *familiar* with the fathers, if you know what I mean. Queenie knew Elsie was looking for a nanny, and she recommended Amelia out of spite. She and Elsie never did get on well because Elsie had no problem standing up to Queenie. If she'd known Queenie had intentionally finagled it so that Amelia became her nanny in the hopes of disrupting Elsie's marriage, I suspect she wouldn't have been too happy with Queenie. It's quite possible she found out."

There wasn't much more to learn, and in due course, Franny took her leave minus the flask. Once she'd gone, Max and Rosemary returned to the dining room where they gave the others the gist of the conversation.

"I didn't notice anything untoward between Amelia and Elsie's husband at the fête." Vera squinted as she played back the scene in her memory. "He barely looked at her, but that could have been purposeful on their part to throw off suspicion."

"Quite likely." Frederick stuck his foot in it. "As Amelia is a woman made to be looked at."

"And I," Vera's voice took on a dark tone as she waved her fork at Frederick, "am one to poke out a man's eye should it stray too far."

"I didn't say she was a woman to touch, did I? After all, one can appreciate a fine painting without needing to cut it from the frame. But you do make a point even if it is not the one you intended." Frederick looked at Rosemary to see if she followed his logic.

"As amusing as I always find Vera's willingness to resort to violence, I do notice she's not threatening the eyes of an innocent bystander, or even a guilty one."

"I don't know that I understand." Evelyn exchanged a look with Stella, who seemed similarly confused. "What does this mean?"

"That if Mrs. Fletcher's husband were to fall prey to Amelia's charms," Max said, his face taking on the slightest tinge of red at having to explain, "she would be more likely to feed him a cup of poison than to take her ire out on Mrs. Baker for setting the possibility in motion."

"Or," Cecil added, "to serve the nanny a cup of doctored tea."

Over after-dinner drinks, speculation continued, and even as she fell asleep, Rosemary considered whether Queenie might have pushed Elsie too far.

CHAPTER TWENTY

Just before teatime on the following day, several cars pulled into the driveway of Woolridge House; fewer than had been expected for the next protection society meeting.

With the specter of murder looming over the group, only Beryl and the four members of Queenie's former entourage had deigned to attend.

Rosemary searched Elsie's face for signs of guilt given she was accompanied by Amelia and Nigel, who'd come to occupy Nelly while the meeting took place. Stella joined Rosemary and Vera, who had agreed to attend to observe what they correctly suspected would become a spectacle.

The fleeting thought that perhaps the Society for the Protection of Euphorbia Villosa might soon become defunct crossed Rosemary's mind. *So much the better*, she thought to herself with a smirk.

Everyone gathered in the entrance hall just as Desmond emerged from the dining room.

"Welcome," Evelyn said, coming in behind him. "Why don't we retire to the solarium?" She made certain to stand between Beryl and Olive, who glared at one another with enough malice to cause the temperature to plummet towards freezing. Evelyn's jaw clenched, but instead of commenting, she merely ushered the women towards the back of the house.

Rosemary hung back, watching Desmond's eyes linger over Amelia before he shook his head as if to clear his thoughts, and then he said politely, "I'd be happy to help track down young Nelly for you. Shall we check the nursery first?"

Amelia blushed and replied softly, "That would be appreciated, thank you."

In a gentlemanly manner, he escorted her up the stairs. Rosemary smiled ruefully, but was, in actuality, relieved that Desmond's romantic intentions now seemed directed elsewhere. She now understood Frederick's comment the evening before, regarding Desmond having become restless as of late. Now, he was one less problem on her plate, and one less obstacle in the way of her possible budding romance with Max.

A weight lifted off her shoulders and put a spring in her step when she entered the solarium, only to discover that the tension in there hadn't waned after the confrontation in the entrance hall. Beryl and Olive stood opposite one another as though they were poised to engage in a duel, while Evelyn attempted to command the front of the room.

Rosemary watched her face as it cycled through a range of emotions, and when Evelyn's jaw clenched, she prepared for a deluge.

"Your attention, please," Evelyn said, tapping on the table with her knuckles. "If we're to continue with this endeavor—one I believe we all feel is worthwhile, otherwise, we wouldn't be here—we're going to have to figure out a way to get along. Now, Olive, I'm terribly sorry that you suspect Beryl of this heinous crime; however, the police have tested the teacup Queenie drank from and determined it contained no poison. Since Beryl had no other opportunity to administer the poison, she's been ruled out as a suspect. Continuing this animosity won't solve anything!"

Olive's face had gone pink, and she interjected sharply, "Your family has the police in their pocket, Evelyn. Everyone knows that. Who's to say Beryl didn't put the poison in something else Queenie might have drunk from? We were all aware of her drinking and knew of the flask she was never without. Perhaps that's how the poison was delivered!"

Vera gave Rosemary a nudge with her arm and whispered, "The flask they vehemently denied having knowledge of just mere days ago? Is that the one she's talking about?"

Olive's statement set the room to twittering, and Beryl's face turned even stormier than before.

"I wouldn't have wasted my time poisoning Queenie; she wasn't worth it," she declared brazenly. "I realize her so-called friends would enjoy pretending she was a peach, but we all know the truth. I don't care what demons she faced; it didn't excuse her actions. I didn't kill her, but I'm not sorry she's dead!"

Another uproar had Olive and Beryl spitting at each other, and the commotion forced Evelyn to bang on the table, harder this time, and practically shout to be heard over the din. "Get a hold of yourselves! Either sit down

174

and have a discussion like adults or leave my home immediately!"

Rosemary exchanged a look with Vera, one of admiration for Evelyn's outburst. "She's not shying away now, is she?"

"I find it rather amusing, to be perfectly honest," Vera replied. "Let these biddies be the target of your mother's ire. I'm thrilled to be on the nice list for once."

Evelyn's outburst broke the tension. Olive, Beryl, and the rest gathered their wits and sat down.

"Now, let's put this whole thing to rest. The poison was not administered to Queenie via the teacup, nor the flask. The police will be back to check the grounds again, and until then, I think we ought to get back to the business at hand."

Settling down proved to be a thing of which none of the women were capable, particularly Olive, who asked in a much softer tone than she'd used previously, "What about the cigarette holder Queenie always carried? She loved that thing; said it made her feel like …" she glanced at Vera and then shifted her eyes away shamefully, "like the lead in a play."

"Actually," Stella spoke up, "the cigarette holder was tested as well. Nelly found it, and we handed it over to the detective inspector."

Minnie's brow furrowed, and her eyes narrowed. "Nelly found it?"

"Yes," Stella explained. "He's at that age where he wants to explore. He's been tearing Woolridge House apart, hiding bits and pieces here and there. I suspect, Elsie, that he and Nigel have dug up all the treasures the grounds have to offer."

"Evelyn, I'd like to use your powder room," Minnie said, rising from her chair. "I'll just be a moment."

"Of course, of course." Evelyn waved her away and prepared to get on with SPEV business but quickly realized that wasn't going to happen.

Elsie swallowed hard, a look of concern covering her face. "I hope the lads are exercising caution. Nigel is somewhat delicate."

Rosemary didn't think *delicate* was an accurate term to describe the husky Nigel, but she declined to comment. Stella, similarly, employed the manners their mother had drilled into their heads since birth.

"I'm positive that between Nan and Amelia, they're just fine," Stella assured her.

Olive mumbled something about Amelia, causing Elsie to whip her head around and glare at her with barely concealed irritation. "What was that, Olive?"

"Nothing," Olive said haughtily. "I just don't know why you'd want that girl in your house, around your husband. Haven't you heard the rumors flying around about her?"

Elsie smiled at Olive, a smile that was both indulgent, as though she were placating a child, and laced with pity. "Amelia is a lovely—albeit sometimes frustrating—girl whose name has been sullied due to the ramblings of insecure women like yourself. My marriage is quite secure, thank you. It's not my husband who's been catting around behind my back!"

Utter silence followed the statement, and once again, Vera and Rosemary exchanged a look of incredulity. Meek little Elsie, who never had a bad word to say about anyone, had just speared Olive with a verbal toothpick.

"It's about to get even uglier," Vera muttered, to which Rosemary agreed.

Olive sputtered and finally spat, "*My* husband would *never* have the gall to step out on me if that's what you're implying!"

"Perhaps not," Elsie said, "but I've seen the way he looks at Amelia—how they *all* look at Amelia. To a man, they're taken in by her charms. It's downright lewd and disgraceful."

"Not *my* husband!" Olive roared. "I blame Minnie for this, just as much as Queenie. She brought destruction on us all when she plotted to get Amelia assigned as your nanny!"

That bit of information was something Elsie evidently hadn't been privy to. Rosemary watched as the realization sunk in and deduced that Elsie's relationship with the rest of the younger set had come to an abrupt end.

"I've had just about enough of the lot of you!" Franny exclaimed, rising from her seat and shaking like a leaf. "You ought to be ashamed of yourselves, speaking ill of the dead like this!"

"And you've always defended her, no matter how malicious her actions," Olive spat back. She continued to sputter, and the insults pinged back and forth across the solarium.

Evelyn had sunk into her chair and could only look around in consternation, but a theory had begun to take shape for Rosemary. She closed her eyes and tried to block out all the noise and, finally, rose to pull Vera off to the side where they could converse without being overheard.

"Vera, I have a terrible feeling I know who did it. I don't have any proof, but think about this: Queenie recommended Amelia as a nanny for Elsie. She didn't know for certain whether anything would come of it, but I get the impression that she had a tendency to plant little bombs here and there. Some were duds, but others hit their marks."

"Seems to have been her way," Vera agreed.

"What if it wasn't Elsie's husband who strayed, but Minnie's instead? You weren't there when I spoke to Minnie, but she did her best to deflect my attentions towards Elsie."

Vera frowned. "I wouldn't have thought Elsie had the nerve for murder."

"Minnie might. She's hard to read, but there's something simmering below that blank surface. She would have been angry with her husband, of course, but she would have been just as angry with Queenie."

"Angry enough to kill her?" Vera looked doubtful, but then, she was more direct in her dealings with people and expected others to be the same.

"Possibly. Anyone can kill if pushed too far, and Minnie assured me Queenie liked to push."

Rosemary rubbed her cheek as she talked it through. "It would have been child's play to pass the murder weapon to Queenie quite innocuously. Then, Minnie could have put the flask back in with Queenie's things to place blame on Franny, and she could have been searching the gardens for the actual murder weapon when she showed up here the other day."

Whatever response Vera might have voiced was cut short by Amelia rushing into the midst of the meeting to announce, "The children. They're missing."

CHAPTER TWENTY-ONE

"Everyone spread out!" Stella demanded, flinging open the doors that led out into the backyard gardens. "Look high and low; Nelly loves to climb."

"What is going on?" Frederick burst into the solarium behind the women, with Desmond close behind. "It sounds like all hell is breaking loose in here!"

"It is," Rosemary tossed over her shoulder. "Nelly and Nigel have run away. We have to find them. There's a murderer in the house! Tell Bertram to call Max immediately!"

Frederick blanched and put on more speed. The search raged for only a few minutes—minutes that felt like hours—until Rosemary heard a voice coming from around the corner of the horse barn. There, perched on the edge of a too-thin-looking branch, was Nelly, his arm outstretched in an attempt to wrest something shiny from the nest of a bird.

On the ground, Minnie clutched Nigel's arm hard enough to send fingernails digging into his skin, and the poor boy did now appear as delicate as his mother believed him to be. Tears streamed down his face, but

Minnie's attention was focused on Nelly.

"Get it and toss it to me. You won't fall. You're a natural climber." There was an edge to her voice and a look of urgency on her face. Rosemary froze; there wasn't anything she could do to help Nelly, not with Minnie standing right there. She contemplated lunging at the woman, but didn't want to hurt Nigel in the process, or startle Nelly so that he fell. Instead, she settled for an attempt at distraction.

"Minnie, what are you doing?" she asked, keeping the edge out of her voice with effort.

Minnie whipped around, releasing her hold on Nigel's arm in the process. He took the opportunity to make a run for it, but his pudgy legs would only carry him so far. He fell at Rosemary's feet, and she stepped in front of him, pushing him gently away from Minnie.

"It's all right, Mrs. Kitteridge," Nelly hollered, oblivious to the danger he was in. "I've almost got it."

"He's almost got what, Minnie?" Rosemary said in the most menacing tone she could muster. By now, the rest of the group had heard the commotion, and they were all running in the direction of the barn.

"The lipstick. He's got the lipstick!"

"That's the murder weapon, isn't it?" Rosemary demanded just as everyone else rounded the corner. Minnie, having been exposed, reared and tried to make a break for it. The commotion startled Nelly, who lost his footing and had to cling to the branch to keep from falling to the ground.

Simultaneously, Beryl lunged at and corralled the spitting Minnie while Amelia kicked off her shoes, hiked up her skirt, and made a mad dash for the tree. Up she climbed, quick as a cat, and somehow managed to hook her legs around the branch to steady herself, grabbing for Nelly at the same time.

Minnie howled and bucked against Beryl while Amelia lowered Nelly down to the safety of his mother's arms. The rest of the group surrounded Minnie like an angry mob, making escape impossible.

"Oh, thank goodness!" Stella cried. "Thank you, Amelia, thank you, thank you, thank you," she repeated, squeezing Nelly so tightly he yelped. Her breath came in short spurts, and when Evelyn approached, she handed Nelly off, stood with effort, and strode towards Minnie. Her eyes were wild with fury, and she looked as though she might take the woman's head off before Frederick grabbed her and held her back.

"You need to calm down, dear sister. The police will handle her. Max is on his way."

That sent Minnie into another fit, and she attempted to lunge at Amelia, who was being tended to by Desmond. "You! This is your fault! I ought to kill you, too, you little—ow!" she yelled when Beryl twisted her arm even tighter.

While that struggle raged, Rosemary pried the prized object from Nelly's fingers. She looked at the treasure he'd risked his life to retrieve, and then back at Minnie, knowing that unless she did something quickly, that woman might escape justice.

Calculating the possibilities, Rosemary saw Max and a constable running across the lawn towards the barn and made a decision.

Max was, fortunately, still out of Minnie's line of sight, and Rosemary sent him a signal to remain there.

With a nod of understanding, Max crept towards the circle where Minnie was being corralled, and just as he got into earshot, she put her last-minute plan into action.

"You were looking for this lipstick, weren't you?" she demanded of Minnie, taking care not to allow her to see what was actually in her hand. "Because it was the only piece of evidence that could have connected you to Queenie's murder. Why did you do it, Minnie?"

With her dander well and truly up, Minnie wanted to confess.

"Because she deserved it! Queenie didn't care who she hurt, so long as it wasn't her feeling the pain. She laughed in my face when I told her the plan to interfere with Elsie's marriage had gone awry. It was *my* husband who was catting around with Amelia, not Elsie's. Queenie found my pain and humiliation quite humorous, but she's not laughing now! And you, Elsie! You had to have known about it, but did you think to let me in on your little secret?"

At that, Elsie's eyes narrowed, and she stepped closer to Minnie. "You've got a lot of nerve, considering you obviously knew what Queenie had planned and didn't say a word of warning to *me*!"

Amelia broke away from her place next to Desmond and joined the fray. "I wouldn't have touched a hair on your husband's head!" she spat. "I'm not that type of girl, despite what people say about me. Is it my fault men find me attractive? Your husband was the worst one of all. Making passes, cornering me when I was alone. Disgusting is what he is! I told him to leave me alone, but he didn't listen. He's the one you should have been angry with. Not me, and not Mrs. Baker!"

Minnie didn't have much to say on the subject, but Max had heard enough. "Minnie Kitteridge, you're under arrest for the murder of Queenie Baker." He handed Minnie off to the constable, and then he peered at Rosemary with a question in his eyes.

She opened her hand to reveal a butterscotch candy, its shiny golden wrapper glinting in the sun. "It wasn't even the lipstick she was after. I expect she'll be rather disappointed when she finds out she would have pulled it off—until her confession, of course."

"Rosemary, you're one in a million," Max praised, giving her shoulder a squeeze. "I'll be back to see you after I've dealt with Mrs. Kitteridge."

He nodded once and then sauntered back across the lawn. Rosemary stared after him, her emotions raging, and told herself it was just the adrenaline.

Once Minnie had gone, Evelyn took control and directed everyone back towards the solarium, where she promised to have the staff serve some soothing tea. Frederick took Vera's arm while Desmond did the same with Amelia, and it was little Nelly who fell into step with Rosemary as they crossed the lawn.

"Auntie Rose, might I possibly have that butterscotch?"

CHAPTER TWENTY-TWO

Max arrived back at Woolridge House later that same evening, exhausted, and needing sustenance after the ordeal of arresting and booking Minnie for murder. Rosemary had a plate brought to him in the garden, and they watched, together, as the sun began its descent below the tree line. Now, the murder having been put behind them, the terrace felt like a piece of home again, and she was able to relax fully for the first time since her arrival in Pardington.

"This cottage pie is delicious," Max commented through a mouthful of tender meat and fluffy potatoes. "Maybe even better than my mother's."

The mention of his mother caused Rosemary to hiccup and Max's eyebrow to raise quizzically. "What?"

"Nothing, really." She tried to push him off, but he continued to press.

"You've been acting oddly ever since our conversation regarding men and their mothers. What is it that has you in a dither? It's *me*, Rose; you can be candid."

There was no part of her that wished to reveal the

thoughts that had been coursing through her head over the last few days. Not one bit did she want to discuss how relieved she'd been when, after the commotion had died down, Desmond had announced he'd become quite taken with Amelia—and she with him. Rosemary sensed a wedding in his future, and she'd whispered congratulations in his ear when he'd embraced her apologetically.

"You deserve to be simply overwhelmed with joy, Des dear," she'd said. "It's a lovely match, and I wish you nothing but the very best. Don't be a stranger."

He'd promised to visit often, and then surreptitiously cleared out of Woolridge House amongst more well-wishes from the rest of the family.

Rosemary turned her attention back to Max, shifted in her seat, and tried to frame a suitable lie. Coming up with nothing, she opted for the truth. "I was concerned, when you said all those things, that it meant if your mother didn't approve of me, it would mean a romance—should we choose to have one—would be doomed. I didn't get the impression that she *did* think very highly of me when we met in London."

Max's expression didn't change, though his eyes did widen at her brazenness. "That's the first time you've admitted that you might have feelings for me," he said. "Do you realize that?"

"I do realize that," Rosemary admitted. "And I can barely breathe right now, waiting for your reaction."

He patted his mouth with his napkin and placed it on the table, turning to Rosemary and taking her hands in his. "I've struggled, I won't lie, with my feelings for you. They feel like a betrayal, even though I know

Andrew wouldn't take it as such. I can only imagine how much more difficult it's been for you, and the last thing I want is to jump into something feet first. I'm willing to take things as slowly as you need to, but there's one thing I can say with certainty: there's nobody like you in the world, Rose. I'm completely enamored."

Max pulled Rosemary to her feet, and there, as the last flickering light of the sun blinked beneath the horizon, he fitted his lips over hers.

Still floating on air an hour later, Rosemary bid Max goodbye with a promise to meet once they'd returned to London and joined the rest of her family in the library for customary after-dinner drinks.

Frederick held Vera's hand tightly while a debate about the fate of the preservation society raged across the room.

"But, Vera dear, if you moved house back to Pardington, you could be my second in command," Evelyn urged.

Vera laughed and said, "I expect you see that as an enticement, and though I appreciate the offer, Evelyn, I don't think relocation is in my future. After having seen what goes on out here in the country, I find the city more civilized."

At that, Evelyn's eyes narrowed to slits, and her mouth pressed into a thin line. *Oh no*, Rosemary thought to herself. *Round two has already begun!*

The End

Printed in the USA
CPSIA information can be obtained
at www.ICGtesting.com
CBHW030856140224
4219CB00099B/984

9 781953 044242